JEREMIAH'S GHOST

JEREMIAH'S GHOST

An Apocalyptic Fantasy

ISAAC CONSTANTINE

MP PUBLISHING

JEREMIAH'S GHOST

First edition published in 2015 by

MP Publishing
12 Strathallan Crescent, Douglas, Isle of Man IM2 4NR British Isles
mppublishingusa.com

Book design by Alison Graihagh Crellin

Publisher's Cataloging-in-Publication data

Constantine, Isaac.
  Jeremiah's ghost : an apocalyptic fantasy / Isaac Constantine.
  p. cm.
  ISBN 978-1-84982-334-0

1. September 11 Terrorist Attacks, 2001 --Fiction. 2. End of the world --Fiction. 3. New York (N.Y.) --Fiction. 4. Tel Aviv (Israel) --Fiction. 5. Fathers and sons --Fiction. 6. Family --Fiction. 7. Fantasy fiction. I. Title.

PS3603.O55795 .J47 2015
813.6 --dc23

ISBN 978-1-84982-334-0
10 9 8 7 6 5 4 3 2 1

Also available in eBook

PART 1

For a poet buys this power
of words to utter all the grim
secrets of others at the cost of
a little secret he himself cannot
utter, and a poet is not an
apostle, he casts devils out only
by the power of the devil.

Johannes De Silentio
Fear and Trembling

CHAPTER ONE
A Little Hysteria

The trouble started before that night at the house in the woods where I lost my mind to the voices, and the shadows grew legs again and dropped from the walls like assassins—but that night it started with Craig.

Craig was an alum who hit it big in the dot-com boom. Craig was lonely and confused, so he threw these "parties" at his spiffed-up log cabin way out on Oblong Road with amber mahogany floors and matching cabinets, for other confused and lonely types. Tonight, like other nights at Craig's, the guests were summer holdouts. Some were undergrads on correctional leave who could think of nowhere better to go for three months; others, like me, even worse, were recent graduates who had done our time, who were free to do anything and live anywhere, but could not motivate ourselves to leave this shitty little town due west of Nowhere, Massachusetts.

Prisoners of habit, we believed we had little in common and less to discuss. No one was introduced. We kept to small familiar groups, or kept to ourselves. People spoke softly as though to protect conversations from prying ears. Watches were checked reflexively though no one had anywhere to be. A few of us dropped acid.

A circle of partygoers drew with magic markers. None of them had taken any drugs, strangely. Splayed on the polished hardwood floor they tried to light a spark in the airless room, coloring quietly, sober and flaccid like bored children. Craig lay on his stomach, propping up his torso with one arm while the other dragged an orange marker down the blank white sheet.

I had become friendly, if not quite friends, with Craig, and something about him was off. There was always something vaguely depressing about him and now it was striking. His eyes were little black coals. His face drooped like Eeyore the Ass.

I was only ten or twenty feet from him when I laughed out loud. I thought he would understand the joke and had a mind to share it. That was my first thought. But Craig never looked up. So I watched him. And I saw his body lying there but knew that he was somewhere else.

Now I start feeling sorry, sorrier as his sadness spreads arms for me. The mystery of the wound he carries fills the space between us. I no longer see his suffering; I am part of it. It annexes my body—spreading, petrifying cell by cell. We share an infection, a heaviness, a dull vibration pulsing through networks of nerves. What I feel is like the very worst I have felt on my worst day, only worse, and I know he carries it always and he sees no end. I never knew what it meant to empathize with someone—not like this. It's horrible.

I find a ride to town and climb the flickering grey stairwell to my summer apartment on Chestnut Street. I can't sleep. Stumbling downstairs again I exit out back and the whirring insectile droning from nowhere that keeps me awake expands outward in the cold summer air, absorbing the crickets, and fills up the night. I hurry past the dumpsters through the empty graveled lot to nowhere in particular. Something follows.

I tell myself I do not hear my name in distant, garbled screams. I tell myself that nothing tripped my legs. "This is all in my head," I say on the ground. I say it out loud like I can trust any voice I hear clearly.

For the first time in weeks I want to be with her. I know she'll be gone for hours, though. And showing up at the theater now? Like this?

So I troll the campus grounds till dawn thinking this is it. This is when the echo chamber in my head implodes and the walls that hold my secrets collapse. My body and mind are only a vessel, a host, and the mask will fall (I, the "I" of me, will dissolve and the ghost of a million tongues will testify). What then? Could anyone empathize? I think they will get the gist at least without my needing to confess. Maybe I'll get help without asking.

Back in bed—waiting, watching the ceiling—I see faces stealing form from shadows. I hear voices crooning and shouting my name. I hear them every night as I drift fitfully to sleep. I remember the things I used to hide from in my room back home, the monsters in the closet, the night shadows and hovering ghosts. I remember the goose lamp; the noises; the deeper shades of darkness groping in the dark. I think of praying.

When Celeste finally arrives (she'd been sewing costumes for a play in the summer festival), she is over and underdressed as usual. Her casual dress would be elegant, formal even as lingerie, my mind observes. Radiant, formidable, she absorbs the sunlight straining through dusty grey blinds; her pale legs bare to the thigh, the sea-green gauze of her mermaid camisole and pale suggestion of breasts enchant the dark blue room. Her eyes aim an accusation at me, like I'm the one who is all tramped up and was gone the entire night. Confidence is her couture, a look of bold determination sparkling like a halo of sequins. I see through it now. I never wanted to look.

My heart beats. My body breathes without me. Moments arrive and depart like jets. She stands by the door like someone waiting for instructions.

For the first time in years I begin to sob. My sobs are heaving, torrential; my whole body clenches, my slightly overgrown nails cut deep red grooves in my palms.

Finally she approaches. Stiletto heels on hollow wood…the perfect legs I've grown so tired of cry out in her black leather skirt, pleading. She stops at the foot of the bed. She sits carefully.

"What is it?"

She expects to hear I fucked someone. I hear it in her voice. Her tone is not one of accusation. Her inflections, though packed with suspicion, lack venom. The words are detached and deflated. Their edges are dulled with tragic acceptance.

I want to confide right now. I know we have to have "the talk" we have always avoided. But what can I say? I'm tired of her? I'm tired of yelling at her?

Can I tell her I'm tired of fighting, of her crying every time we fight, or when her director yells at her, or if she gets turned down for a job, or if I'd rather not eat pizza on a night she craves it? That no matter how hard she works to embellish the femme fatale costume she wears, underneath she is so fragile I can't imagine getting through one more month with her, let alone through the rest of our lives? Would it help to say it? To have it said? Would the truth set us free?

Can I tell her she doesn't turn me on so much anymore, though many, many women do? That things have grown so dull I've just about run out of people I know to pretend to be fucking instead of her? Or how, as I have pounded and bruised her up from behind, I have sunk so low as to desecrate her supple flesh with the head of Jill Rogan, a certain psychotic bitch she and I have grown to love to hate together, the thrill of complicity igniting our last sparks of lust? Would it cushion the blow to hear I still love her, sort of, on some level, albeit some gelded mutation of love that will fail to replicate and die? Should she know she is still the most beautiful?

"I tripped," I say. "I'm still tripping."

She says nothing.

"Craig…I-I…I was watching him and…he…he was so…sad. So miserable. I felt him. God…"

It's enough. In one slow, graceful turn she crawls up the bed; she cradles my head in her lap, my weight shifts and I turn facedown to meet her. Beneath the perfume and leather, in the sea-breeze musk of buried skin, I find her as Bishop found the ocean: cold, dark, deep, absolutely clear. My head retreats deeper in the leather cocoon, between her thighs. I absorb her sighs sinking, expanding forever to blue-black horizons. Humming into the void my song becomes hers, exploding to the surface, and now I could just let go and merge with her. I could dissolve in the taste of her. Almost.

"Celeste is gonna flip the fuck out when she finds out I'm tripping again." The tab had dissolved on my tongue. I spat the chewed-up pulp at the gate to the meadow on Red Rock Hill.

"Why?" Small squinted his wide blue eyes at me. He studied me close.

"Last week." Craig's Crayola bash was the weekend before.

"Oh, right. Your little breakdown."

"It didn't seem so little then." The fucker. "I got inside Craig's head," I pursued, punctuated with three stiff knocks to mine. "It *pulled* me in. And it really sucked in there. It was awful."

And it was, but it was more that he got stuck in mine. I couldn't stop thinking about that night—the oppressive vibe at the party, Craig's sad face, the anxiety that haunted me through the next morning with Celeste. I remembered that feeling now, and before I decided to trip again. And yet.

"That sounds kinda cool," Small said. "I like that sad acid underbelly."

I lit a Parliament. Small waited. *THERE'S NOTHING FREER THAN A DEAD DOLPHIN* announced his double-extra-large t-shirt, which he'd painted himself. A graceful giant, all six feet two inches and two hundred and ninety pounds of him seemed to hover and glide in his size thirteen sandals along Route 6. We were headed to Chestnut, the only street in town where anyone did anything, and then not much. The old sign loomed ahead in purple and puce with bold white type:

Johnston College
Strive Boldly
Bound for Excellence:
for the Moon, the Stars
and the Hours Hence.
Commemoratum Rememberatum
Est. 1796

"Do you mind when you're lying in bed," I said, finally, "and the room starts crowding in on you, and you feel like someone's holding you down? Do you like hyperventilating? Or tossing in cold sweat while shadow faces stare you down on the ceiling?"

"I dunno. Were they friendly shadow faces?"

We shared a laugh.

"You should have come by my place then," Small offered, the comment now obsolete. "I was up, too. And Celeste wouldn't be much help in that situation."

"No," I said. "She was not." But thanks, I could help myself.

I chose to sit one step above Small on the post office steps, where we sat and watched cars pass up and down the town's only commercial block, along with a few locals, students and theater-bound tourists. The smell of fresh-cut grass waxed and waned in tidal rhythmic gusts. The pavement blazed in sunlight; heat beat down on our heads, so we sat and waited for dusk, and suddenly the temperature dropped ten degrees and the light was soft and lavender as the sun flashed a final gaze in the storefront windows. They were prettier than life, the concrete and red-brick buildings smooth and glowing like a townscape painting or set backdrops.

A pack of tennis campers in shorts and Nike t-shirts marched to the ice cream shop. Two blondes trailed behind. Their nubile asses bucked on slender legs.

Something must have been off. In the past LSD had softened

urges of the flesh, diverting my mind toward loftier, spiritual-type yearnings.

"Look at that," I said.

"Yeah?"

"Shit must be like twelve years old. If that."

I laughed.

"I just hope I'm not still looking when I'm fifty, you know?" I continued, unprompted. "I don't wanna be that guy. How do you prevent that kind of thing?" The question had been rhetorical.

"Stop looking now," he said.

And I guessed he was right, but it was everywhere, and I loved to look. It was all that sustained me on my route for Office Services, where I served as Interdepartmental Mail Carrier for all of Johnston College, or what remained of it over the summer. Ass and being outside all day were what made the job tolerable. Like candy, it came in all sizes and wrappings, treats for all the mindless repetition of sorting and hauling sacks of eight-by-eleven yellow envelopes sealed with red strings.

I had taken the job before the summer, with some hesitation, to be near Celeste while I wrote, or pretended to write. Now I regretted my choice and resented the work. I was ashamed to be tooling around all day with a mailbag over my shoulder leering at ass like some townie high school dropout.

And the town was tiny, and it was impossible to avoid seeing, and being seen by anyone. Just that morning I saw Jill Rogan, my friend-turned-nemesis and fantasy hate-sex partner. She saw me, too. I crossed Chestnut when she drove by and shot a hateful condescending smile.

The war broke out one afternoon the previous winter. The opening salvos burst at Dexter Hall—a.k.a. "the Dirty Dex," a.k.a. "the Dirty"—where we ate most of our meals senior year. Jill and I began lunch as friends. She, Celeste, two other friends, and I sat at a table along the wall of the curved interior (the Dex, erected in the late sixties, was round with curving windows and a conical shingled roof). Jill had been the editor of *The Low Down*, an alternative campus "newspaper"/tabloid that Celeste and I both wrote for and helped edit, too. The task of running the rag grew heavy on Jill, as she complained frequently. Near the end of first semester, Jill, after weeks of agonizing—often public—indecision, determined that she was unable to manage the paper on top of her senior-year course load, and resigned in a rapid fire of anguished, defensive emails to the *Low Down* listserv.

Which left the future uncertain for the beloved *Low Down*, and for the surviving staff. No one expected to step in for Jill and no one was prepared. But Tom Grimes and other alum friends of ours had started the paper the year before; they graduated and left it to us and we wanted to keep it alive. So Celeste and I decided to run it together, dividing Jill's responsibilities between us. And we got lots of praise. Congratulations poured through the listserv from former and current staff. Everyone was happy except Jill.

"I just feel like now everyone's all, 'Hurray for Celeste and Jeremiah,'" she told us across the lunch table. "And that's great, except what about all the work I did for months running everything alone, or basically?"

It was too much.

"I get it, Jill." My voice rose. "Before you were upset because no one wanted you to leave, and now you're sour because no one kissed your ass enough before you left, or after. Is that it?"

Her face trembled. "I gave *everything* to that paper. For Tom and *everyone* else." She coughed her words through tears. She stood, grabbed her tray, and left.

She had worked hard.

I made what I considered an effort at damage control, and wrote Jill an email later that day. I apologized but also defended my side of the argument (in truth more lines by far were dedicated to the defense than to the apology). She never responded, though she attacked me in another email a week later on some pretense. It escalated to a four-month email war with battles erupting at intervals between tense and hate-filled silences.

Celeste got involved, too. Once she called Jill "ugly." She seemed to have fun with it all, Celeste did. She smiled when she related what she'd said to Jill, and Jill's gasping, enraged reaction. She spoke quickly, excited and pleased with herself. And I smiled too, but there was much more to hating Jill than fun and romance.

I never knew I was capable of the hatred I felt for Jill. The force of it surprised and overwhelmed me. It ruined the second half of senior year—hers and mine. It smoldered for months in me, exploding on her with the slightest test.

The hate was palpable, literally, an infection with bodily symptoms. It tensed my limbs, my shoulders and neck. It altered and amplified my heart's rhythms. Each morning I woke with chest and stomach pain and it only got worse. The thought of her blackened my mood instantly. She entered and inhabited my mind as though it were her own, unearthing rage, bloodlust, and warlike instincts buried deep and now tearing at the flesh, portending another new and old and terrible layer of "me."

And the new me (we'll call him "he," or "him") hated other people, too. Campus security officers; small-town cops; his landlord, Bob; the librarian with flipper arms who denied him access to the AV room and archives after graduation (she invoked "school policy," even as he delivered the bitch her mail)—he hated them all, or hated them more for hating Jill. The new Jeremiah cringed and clenched whenever he left his room on the chance of seeing her. He did not experience the panoply of human emotion from one feeling to the next with a million subtle shades and tones. He brooded mostly; otherwise he hated or craved.

The spring was almost over and graduation only weeks ahead when a handle of bourbon—property of the *Low Down* staff—disappeared from Celeste and Jill's shared common room. That's when this new Jeremiah shot over an email informing Jill that she was "a friendless…hideous bitch" and threatening her in no uncertain terms with some unspoken act of violence.

"You okay there, Jeremiah?"

"What? Oh, yeah. I was just thinking about Rogan." My face must have shown it. "I saw the cunt today. On my route." Then, as an afterthought, "First time all summer—kind of a small miracle in this town."

Jill hung back that summer, too, for God knows what. She was renting a place on the outskirts of town, where she lived with her boyfriend, Dwight, a tall, bald computer whiz who hated me, too, though no more than I hated his turtlenecks or his stupid goatee.

"Jesus, forget Jill," said Small. "She's just crazy."

"I know she's crazy," I said. "She's fuckin' nuts. But she's hard to forget."

"I can't believe you two still hate each other so much."

But we did, and we would for a long time.

The grudge would live five long years. Jill and I would finally pass each other on the street in New York the year before my wedding. A transit strike would cripple the city before Christmas; I'd walk with my fiancée over the Brooklyn Bridge downtown to shop for a new pair of jeans, and down near Canal, beneath the makeshift blue wooden boards of a sidewalk construction barrier, our eyes would meet, Jill's and mine, and we'd all keep walking.

Three weeks later I would send her one last email, seeking peace, apologizing once more, this time more gracefully. She had begun to make a name for herself, publishing a variety of articles and interviews in vanguard New York journals, first online and then in print. I was happy for her.

Jill would return an apology. Her email would be friendly, good humored, even self-deprecating. And I think we forgave each other.

One night a few months later Jill would lie down for bed, and due to "as yet unexplained natural causes" (that's what it said when you Googled her name), Jill never woke up again.

What happened next was strange. After the shock, after the sadness and relief, I loved her again. I loved Jill like the friends we once were, except we knew each other and ourselves much better now, and we were closer. I prayed for her, and we touched each other, and held each other suspended in cottony clouds—suspended in time—and naked as birth in gentle stillness. Some nights I spoke to her. I asked where she was, what it was like and what, if anything, she missed. I asked for information on my enemies, and about myself (I needed her help somehow, I believed), and I could swear Jill answered.

The sun set on Johnstontown. The acid turned out pretty mellow, or so far at least. I felt somewhat alert as Small and I discussed our plans.

Small, who didn't read much, was writing a novel. I'd read a few pages of the thing; assaulted by meta-digressions and allusions to books I was certain he had never read, I surrendered. He planned to "publish" it in the fall after nine grueling months of authorship between classes and bong rips. Maybe he considered it his "baby" literally.

The *ignorance*. I recognized it, but couldn't get past the audacity of it, which stung like an insult.

I hadn't written a word in months.

My plan was to return to India in the fall, where I'd lived and studied for one semester my junior year. It wasn't much of a plan, really—just to go back and drift for a year, more or less. I would scribble around in my journal. Maybe I'd find something to write.

There were two problems.

First, I doubted my mental fortitude for extended travel, and India made me extra nervous. Of course that was also the thing that intrigued me most. My experience there had been profoundly disorienting. Everything about the place— the crowds, the noise, the heat, and a thousand other things happening together all at once—overwhelmed me. To live there was to be lost, and in love with losing one's way, and one's self. It infused the air, whatever it was: that vital *feeling*. It was no single feeling at all, but the sum of all feelings combined ecstatically like an explosion. Then I went home, and the feeling was gone. I wanted it back.

But maybe the demons were stronger in places like India, old places with blood-soaked histories where the dead pile up and linger for thousands of years. Maybe there they could enter my dreams, enter my body and strangle me. My nightmares had been terrible when I first arrived there years before. One night I dreamt of a shadowy assassin infiltrating my room, or my much fancier dream room (the ninja scaled a palace wall to reach me; my homestay home was nice for Rajasthan, but certainly no palace), and I woke up trying to strangle myself with my bare hand. But that may just have been my malaria pills.

The second problem was that I was supposed to leave in the next six weeks, and Celeste very likely harbored delusions that she and I would stay "together." We'd never discussed it.

"Hey there? Jeremiah," said Small. "You were saying something?"

"Huh?"

"Yeah, man. You started talking about India. Remember?"

"Oh, yeah…"

Small shifted his weight on the step. His massive head now faced me squarely so his big blue eyes could size me up. "You do that shit a lot. You're always trailing off, or just taking forever to say what you're thinking."

"Maybe that's because we're always tripping, or stoned," I offered.

"Nah. No excuse. You just gotta focus. You're always making people wait, like building suspense. Like it's always something really smart you have to say. You just gotta spit it out. Shit, or get off the pot."

"Wow, Small." Fat fuck. "I wish I could take you with me everywhere. Like a big fat Bodhisattva in a magic lamp."

The measured click of heels alerted me. Celeste wore her miniskirt with the slit halfway to the waist, a pink tank top, bright lip gloss ("Paris Pink") and open-toed pink shoes like frames for a shiny pink pedicure. Her bed was lined with pink stuffed animals. In the winter she wore a faux-fur pink hat, and sometimes a pink fur coat. She often ate Lucky Charms for breakfast, lunch or dinner; she'd spoon out the pink marshmallows first and save them on her plate for last in little milk puddlets. We called her Pinky her freshmen year. That wasn't all we called her.

She walked, or strutted our way, and her eyes were fixed on me. The muscles in her face worked hard, unsuccessfully, to suppress a smile. The mouth was straight but her eyes gave her away. I wondered about this black widow, maneater act of hers, and whether she knew how much it was undercut by her love of pink.

I was happy as she approached; peripherally I was aware of Small, the prime spectator in our act. She liked to make these entrances into the dining hall, or the student lounge, or the library—mostly everywhere. She'd swagger in all noir like Jessica Rabbit, thrusting and bobbing. A stage would appear where none had been, where no one expected a show and where people would notice. She worked me while she worked the crowd, my natural-born performer.

Sad sewer of costumes, beautiful drama queen, master of living street theater, why did you quit the stage? You would have found your role in time. Backstage was never for you. It was never your place to shine, love of yesterday. You should never have stopped acting.

Celeste was driving. It was dark. I sat up front with her and Small was packed in the rear of my red Saturn like a trout in a sardine tin. I'd asked her to drive Small and me to pick up some food. We weren't hungry at all. Still, it was "dinner time," and eating seemed like the thing to do for Celeste's sake, to keep her safe from our secret. Small could always eat.

I wouldn't risk driving, though, so when I asked Celeste to

drive I thought she must have guessed something was up (I wasn't drunk, and she knew I drove stoned all the time). She seemed to play along. Her eyes scolded us playfully. I imagined I saw it whenever she turned to me in the passenger's seat. My heart skipped beats and I'd tell her to watch the road. Several times I thought we'd breached the yellow lines, or a car in front of us stopped short as the taillights flashed and grew larger. I'd yell out; she'd stare back all perplexed and I'd yell at her to watch the road again.

Small and I bought sandwiches at the pizza place on the edge of town. Celeste ordered nothing there. It would be misleading to call her eating habits "picky," or "finicky"; both would understate the nature of Celeste's extraordinary relationship with food. She simply would not eat something she didn't "feel like eating," otherwise she'd "feel all gross" and be "grumpy all day," and what made her grumpy and gross included most foods most days. So on the way back we stopped at the gas station for her dinner—Sweet Tarts, Twizzlers, and a can of Cherry Sprite.

We sat in my apartment, Small and I on reclining chairs and Celeste on the couch. *Saint Matthew Passion* blared on my mini Bose, my own bizarre choice. We sipped, and munched our meatball subs. No one spoke.

"I think we should tell her," Small said, finally. The mood had become too weird even for him.

"Tell me what?" She looked at Small, then stared straight back at me.

"Oh, she knows," I said with mock certainty.

"What?"

"That we're tripping, babe—now. You knew that, right?"

Seconds passed quietly.

"No," she said. "I didn't."

I sat with Celeste on the bed. Small had gone home. I felt lucid, clearer than I had in weeks. I felt like I knew what to say to her, finally, after months of stalling and confusion. Freedom beckoned close. It whispered to me like a woman outside my door, and I was elated, just so pleased with myself and my life in that very moment I felt I could say anything, that anything I said would be sincere and from the heart and as such she could not fail to understand and respect it.

So calmly, with the detached wisdom of a great Zen master of love, I explained. I explained that although tripping two weekends back-to-back might appear reckless, even self-destructive given the way she'd found me the week before, that was only a setback, a pang of the suffering necessary for growth.

I explained how acid was different from other drugs. It awakened dormant faculties inherent in our being—primal, instinctive powers of knowing repressed over thousands of years of "civilization." It broke through inhibitions, barriers that divided us.

If not for the acid, I might never have found the words for what I was about to say to her, I said, which I'd wanted to say for weeks but hadn't yet found the courage to say: it made no sense for us to stay together once I left for India. The distance would be too much.

"I know," she said. "Of course I knew."

"So why haven't we talked about it? Why didn't you say something?"

"What did you want me to say?"

Who could predict my truth would only upset her more?

I caressed her patiently; her sobs grew louder. I wrapped her in my arms and soon she was screaming.

"Celeste, stop."

The temperature dropped. I was cold, awash in her grief. The noise was terrible and soon it was difficult to separate her panic from mine.

"Stop it!" I grabbed her shoulders, gave her one good shake. She was quiet. "Celeste, you have to stop. You're putting me in a bad place now."

It seemed like something had occurred to her. She looked startled.

"What is it?" I said.

She wouldn't speak. I assumed whatever she felt was too much for the words at her command, so I waited. I was getting impatient, though. I wanted to enjoy the rest of my trip.

"We can talk about this later if you—"

"There," she said. She was looking down at herself.

"What?"

"On my arms. Around my body. I can't…feel."

"What do you mean?"

"I can't feel anything. Something's covering me."

I saw nothing.

"It's there," she said. "It wasn't there before."

"What are you talking about?"

I felt the straining of her mind, stretching to grasp familiar words for things she never talked about or needed to describe. "You can't see it," she said, "but it's there. It's both physical and… metaphysical."

Fear gripped my stomach then. Something new and terrible was happening here, in this nowhere town, in this old relationship with a woman I no longer loved to love. This was why I stayed. I was certain of it. I had no clear sense of what was happening to her, or to us, but I sensed it all meant something big for me and I'd probably write about it.

I ushered her through the apartment and out the door. When I touched her, I pulled back my hand real fast. Did I feel something?

I decided to take her to Small. It was the obvious choice.

He brought her into his room and shut the door. I wanted to go in with them as much as I didn't—but as we entered the apartment and everyone looked at each other like we all knew what the matter was, with nothing said besides Small's "Celeste, what's wrong?" I felt I should stay out.

I sat at the kitchen table with Damon, Small's roommate. We were in the same class, though Damon's scrawny frame and prepubescent smoothness made him look real young. He could have been a teenager except for the world-weary hang of his face, which in Damon's case looked genuine, or based on real experience. Then there was the glare in his eye that lit up now and then, flashing the shrewd and slightly unnerving intelligence of a published mathematical "genius"—a triple major with comp sci. and chemistry, with a talent for engineering LSD, which he cooked in the lab at night to sell to students, and some professors, too, though Damon no longer took acid. His failure to graduate for ignoring the school's PE requirement seemed only to brighten his aura of brilliance.

"How did those tabs work for you?" he said. "I made that batch a few days ago. No reports yet—Small likes them, anyway. And what the fuck happened to her?"

The walls and counters were covered in Small's artwork: fingerpaint on a canvas of news clippings, shoebox dioramas and macaroni sculptures. I explained what I could.

"That's why I don't fuck with the stuff," he said. "People aren't meant to see those things."

Then he said something about mushrooms mutating the brains of foraging apes and turning them more human. I could believe anything now, and I wondered aloud if the trip had somehow infected Celeste. Damon said it wouldn't surprise him. From what I could tell, nothing did. He believed FDR sanctioned the attack on Pearl Harbor, and could talk for hours about the "true" motivations behind World War II—something about tobacco, I think—all of which had escaped every historian but those who published exclusively on the Internet, or maybe in California (Damon was from San Mateo). I heard through Small that Damon thought the Johnston Jewish Alliance was in league with the CIA, the Mossad, or both, though to what end I never cared to ascertain.

But here the evidence was hard to ignore. I was sober now—too sober, I thought. And Celeste? The drug, the energy, whatever *it* was, had jumped.

The smell of the place, though never fresh, was suddenly unbearable. The trash in the kitchen vied with the cigarette butts piled three-weeks high in a green sand pail on the table.

I was tense; my heart was still racing and the smell made it harder to breathe. "I've got to get out of here," I said. "I need to be outside."

"Go ahead."

"But I guess I should be here when she gets out. No?"

"Small seems to think he knows what he's doing," he said. "I'm sure she'll be fine."

Damon went on about one time the year before when he was sick and Small "healed" him. Damon had been shaking, shivering, soaking his sheets in cold sweat and puking for days, he said, and no one at the health center or the hospital in West Haven knew what it was. They gave him ultrasounds to check for parasites; they tested his blood and stool and found nothing. They sent him home with all kinds of antibiotics and antiviral pills, he said, but he just got sicker.

Small came by one day to check on Damon (he found him much more miserable, much paler and thinner than usual) and offered a more traditional approach to medicine. Loath to waste precious time and resources, Small skipped the whole diagnostic phase and cut to the chase with a shamanistic miracle cure involving a baby alligator tail—which Small ordered in bulk from Puerto Rico—and a little pouch of gray powder. He told Damon to keep the tail in his pocket and sprinkle the powder in a glass of water twice a day until he got better. In three days the symptoms were gone.

Three or four months later, after the Towers fell, the flags rose, and the firebombs and anti-aircraft party flares lit up the skies over Kabul for days on CNN like a grand celebration; after anthrax spread through the mail, nuclear winter flirted with Kashmir and Jerusalem and I cancelled my trip to India and stayed back home in New York (I left her in Johnstontown; she shacked up with Small and I did my best to pretend not to care)—that's when I started to miss Celeste. Because what was a little hysteria?

CHAPTER TWO
Burning the Monster

It was like the sweet sixteen and the debutante ball he'd never had—that first great literary job straight out of college. Technically, it would not be a "job," but an "internship." Maybe they wouldn't be "paying" him. Perhaps he would forgo the luxury of his own office (as it turned out he would have no cubicle either, or even a desk, though at least one plastic chair would always be empty for him). But, in the words of Mastercard, the opportunity would be priceless. What fool would choose a desk and a few dollars an hour over, say, an apprenticeship at the Globe backstage with Marlowe and Shakespeare? It was kind of like that.

And though Jeremiah had never read or seen an issue of *The New World Quarterly*, its reputation alone made him esteem its name above that of any journal. The little magazine—operated entirely from the Upper East Side brownstone of "Literary Monster" Henry Maxwell—had for half a century published and interviewed all of the greatest writers who lived.

The NWQ was committed as well to "fostering new talents" and "giving voice to new voices." It was all right there on the website with a click on "the mission" tab in the submenu of the "history" page. And the journal devoted a whole issue to first fiction and poetry one fall—the fall of 1988, maybe, and before in the spring of '73. At that rate they'd be due for another soon.

Either way, he could be patient now. One day Jeremiah would write his books and assume his rightful place in the canon. In time his marbled head would perch alongside the heads of his forebears. Chaucer, Dante, Shakespeare, Quixote, Goethe, and, last but not least, the young Levi—ageless and immaculate.

Jeremiah climbed a flight of steps in procession with three editors. He stretched and straightened his legs all the way with each step, which helped with the trembling. They stopped at the top of the stairs to the second floor and Tracy, the managing editor, knocked on a door that was open a crack.

"Yes."

"Henry, it's Tracy."

The door opened, revealing a tall and slender—though broad, imposingly built—and clearly once handsome white-haired gentleman. He wore a navy blue jacket with a button-down and a dark red tie.

"Henry," Tracy said. "This is Jeremiah. He's here for an interview."

"Oh, *yes*," said Henry in that anachronistic, blue-blood drawl Jeremiah mistook for an English accent. It was like Henry had been expecting him, as though he were fully immersed in the journal's daily minutia down to the hiring of interns. This touched Jeremiah more than he would have admitted. "Hello," he said, "Henry Maxwell," extending a large, wrinkled hand.

Jeremiah puffed out his chest, took the hand. "Jeremiah Levi," he said, raising his voice just above the normal pitch of conversation, which embarrassed him. He often tried to compensate for nervousness with a show of self-possession. He relaxed a little when Tracy laughed.

They called Maxwell the "Literary Monster." It came from a book Henry wrote about his pre-season training with, and stint playing third substitute goalie for, the Manitoba Monster, an NHL expansion team from the sixties and seventies.

The moniker was misleading. It wasn't like Jeremiah expected Henry to scream at them all when the door opened, but the man who greeted them surpassed every vague expectation he took to the interview that day. Henry seemed to epitomize gentleness. He was gracefulness and decorum personified. He was no monster.

They left Henry in his office and walked down the hall and around a corner to a great big parlor with large windows framing a lovely view of the East River. The room was lavished with shelves of old books, prints, tribal masks, a polished black Steinway grand, an amber Brunswick Hawthorne American Billiards table with red felt and several horned and antlered heads impaled on placards. The trophies betrayed no fear or dismay, as one might expect in the faces of creatures that died with bullets lodged in their flanks and lungs, coughing up bone splinters. Despite the ordeal they looked dignified, proud even of their sacrifice.

That alone should have given him strength. If Henry's stewardship could inspire these noble beasts to face death with composure, then he, Jeremiah, should have nothing to fear in the modest trial he faced. They sat behind the pool table in a circle of high-backed leather chairs. Jeremiah decided to sit with his hands on his knees. Later his wrists would be stiff and his fingers sore from the clenching.

He was sure he'd fucked up the interview. He'd neglected to think of questions to ask his inquisitors before, predictably, they prompted him. But he got the job somehow. He supposed he *had* had interesting things to say—insightful things. A clever remark he'd made at the expense of David Foster Wallace drew chuckles from all three editors (Jeremiah pretty much idolized DFW, though he knew somehow that he should not).

Weeks later he learned the only other candidate for his job had never bothered, as Jeremiah had, to read the *Quarterly* before his interview. When they asked him why, the guy said he'd looked for a copy everywhere. Which was totally stupid, of course, and seemed like a lie outright until Jeremiah learned the *Quarterly*'s circulation had bottomed out and remained below six thousand an issue for over ten years. Subscribers accounted for half the copies printed. They just happened to have it at Jeremiah's local Barnes and Noble.

Jeremiah liked reading "slush" about suburban swingers, dogs, and psychic prostitutes that helped police solve crimes. Some of the stories he read were bad enough to entertain, and each and every day he'd have something awesomely bad to share with Pablo and Nina, the other interns.

Nina read all the poetry submissions in the slush. She told him every third poem coming in was about September 11th. She was glad they wouldn't surface on the pile for another three months. By then she would have returned safely to Brown. Nina took leave to live in New York for just the wrong semester.

Jeremiah wondered at these fools who believed they had something to say about this cataclysmic shock to the world that had hit just two months before, which no one could possibly have begun to process yet since everyone was still in shock. You could see it in the faces on the street, and he felt it on his own: that tight mask of worry. But it wasn't fear he felt in the moments he watched the Towers fall, not exactly. And it wasn't like it did not, or would not, register, either, as he heard so many claim. He knew exactly what was happening as it happened.

He did not feel like he was "watching," or "in a movie." He wouldn't even call what he felt "dreamlike" or "surreal," since it was more horrible and intense, and so it was realer than anything he could remember feeling in his waking life, let alone in dreams. He was six miles north on the Upper West Side when his father woke him at some ungodly hour to tell him terrorists had crashed two planes into the Trade Center.

"This means war, kiddo," said his dad, like he'd better suit up and report to kill Muslims. They'd better have been big fucking planes, Jeremiah thought, battling the first pangs of consciousness, for his father to wake him weeks before he had a job, and no reason at all to be up well before nine. When he stumbled to his parents' living room, fumbled with the remote, and saw the rivers of fire and smoke devouring the steel fortress where his father worked years before, where Jeremiah played as a boy and slid down the escalators and looked up at the ceilings in the lobby and sometimes even got a little dizzy and scared of the size of it, and if he stood outside, right below them, raised his chin and stretched out his neck to look up, he'd get so scared and dizzy he felt he could slip and fall all the way to the top—seeing what he saw on his parents' thirty-six-inch Mitsubishi screen that morning was shocking, "literally," like volts of electricity. He was painfully aware of every part of his body. His attention sunk to his midsection on down to the base of his spine—Ground Zero—where the shock focused. Then the first tower fell, the volts amped up, and he felt the world ending.

It was shock that gave way to fear as he hurried to the elevator, which his father felt minutes before when he called again to tell Jeremiah to run to the A&P for cans of Progresso soup, boxed fettuccini, and bottles of Poland Spring, and the ten thousand other shoppers felt too as they bumped and tripped around and waited in line while the black cashier lady sermonized and berated them all for shopping when they should have been at home, praying. After she rang and bagged up each of the six-dozen shoppers in Jeremiah's line, the lady said, "Have a nice day. Go home. Pray." When she said it to him he wanted to ask what fuck she was doing at work still, then. But he said nothing.

The fear stayed thick in the air of the city for months, and it started with shock, and no one still in it could know or understand or even remember enough to write about what shocked them and how, since the memories brought back the worst of it—that feeling—and no one really wanted to relive and feel all that again. Not yet. And if you just so happened to be in Montana when it hit, and you weren't that shocked, but you felt compelled to wrap the fresh catastrophe in a tidy ribbon of platitudes, Jeremiah was less than interested.

One of the scariest moments came several weeks after. Late one afternoon, after work, Jeremiah stopped at B&N to read in the café upstairs. There he raced toward the impossible end of *The Infinite Jest*—which had taken him months—with that great drug scene, and the harrowing doomsday plot of French Canadian wheelchair terrorists wielding lethal video cassettes, more harrowing since he could no longer remember or imagine reading any other book. And with less than five long pages to go, the sixty-something-year-old man who sat across from him at the table they shared said, "Whatcha readin'?" The guy had a big hooked nose like a beak. He wore a wool hat with brown ears and a lined beige coat he'd worn for like seventy winters.

Jeremiah resented the question on so many levels. For one, he was "reeedin'," not talkin', so unless you were a hot nineteen-year-old there was nothing at all to discuss. Then it was obvious the guy had no interest in talking about the book, or anything remotely interesting. Soon he wanted Jeremiah's name, where he was from and how old he was. Then came the doddering discourse on the great messianic prophets. Did Jeremiah realize who…?

Yes, he knew where his name came from.

Had he read the book?

No, but he knew enough to pretend he'd read "parts."

Which had been a mistake, clearly, since the ancient ptero-dactyl got all excited and cooed on about the stark beauty of the images, and his syrupy, solicitous eyes locked down on Jeremiah. He recommended Daniel, too.

"What's the trouble?" he asked Jeremiah.

"What trouble?"

"How old are you?"

"Twenty-three."

Then this prehistoric creature nodded to himself and said the thing that scared Jeremiah.

"You have many worries for a man so young."

So here was this old schlepper camping out in Barnes and Noble, sprouting clots of brown fuzz from his nostrils, in a city of shocked and worried people, interrupting his reading to say that he, Jeremiah, looked more worried than he should. Which should have pissed off Jeremiah too, he guessed. On some level it had. But the guy was right. Jeremiah knew his troubles grew from roots far deeper than 9/11.*

Dismissing the man as a proselytizer and Jesus freak, which he was (he kept inviting him to attend his Bible group), proved insufficient. The incident stuck in Jeremiah's mind for months and reminded him of his life's mysterious burden. But how did he know, the nosy old fucker? And what was the matter with him—Jeremiah?

He arrived at the office early the next morning. Nina was there alone. She looked panicked as he climbed the last three spiral steps down to the basement.

"What's wrong?"

"Another plane blew up over Queens. Sally just called."

"What? Is it terrorists?"

"They don't know yet." One tear rolled down her cheek. "I need a hug" she said.

He caught her in his arms. He felt strange, and a little embarrassed at first, though better the longer they stayed.

"Hmm…you give good hugs," she said.

They lingered there. Her long dirty-blonde hair smelled like honeydew, lemongrass. He stole a glance over her shoulder down at her plump little ass in her jeans. "You too."

But Nina was dating Sally, a forty-year-old woman who lived down on the Lower East, and when Jeremiah and Nina hung out once or twice after work all she talked about was Brown, Anne Sexton, and the massive crush she had on Tracy.

Besides, he lived with his parents. Where could he take her?

Months later, when he had his own place, the night Jeremiah thought about ending his life, he remembered the old man in Barnes and Noble. He wondered if the man had been his last hope, if God had extended a hand to him and, having refused it, Jeremiah had finished digging the grave that called to him that night on the Brooklyn Bridge.

---

*The attacks would be a footnote in his *Infinite Jest* of errors.

The night began hopefully, with a sense of purpose. He had plans to meet a friend from college and some of her friends for drinks downtown at Bowery Ballroom. In his mind he seduced them all—inspired, possessed of the muses of language and literature. He practiced several conversations on the subway ride from work.

But once he entered the crowded room, he had nothing to say. When he spoke anyway, if prompted to speak, it was like Jeremiah had switched off his personality to play the sounds of prerecorded voices at the same frequency. It sounded like him; words formed in his throat and slipped from his lips, but he was watching from far away.

The absence of the Towers crested up behind him over the bridge. That dreadful black wave stalked him walking home. He felt it at his back—the void—and knew it would crash down and swallow him. Wind burned his ears and nose. It sprayed the salt and dead-fish smell from Fulton Market over the harbor. His eyes searched everywhere for something unexpected. Just what did he expect—or not expect—to find on these dark perambulations? He asked himself that sometimes. The answer he got was *everything; nothing in particular.* At the first lookout he stopped and his gaze stretched off toward the light, toward midtown and the skyline's frail remains.

Whatever he could have done, whatever he should have done and hoped to do with his life, he had failed. And the world was ending now, or it was beginning to end, and he had nothing to show for it. The old man had Jesus, at least. Jeremiah could mock him, but the old man would not die alone. Where was Jesus now? Jeremiah did not see Him.

All you need to do is ask, said the voice of another woman from college. Never, he thought. And it wasn't that he was a Jew either, or not just. Though tempting, her promise was ominous. Like once you let this Jesus guy out of the lamp, could you put him back in?

Jeremiah never asked for His help that night. Jesus did not keep him on the bridge. No passion at all saved him so much as profound dispassion. He had felt his energy drained a little each day and night—on the miserable, jam-packed morning and evening subway commutes; at work; in his Brooklyn studio, tossing and turning and soaking the sheets; in dreams of snipers' bullets ripping through his skull and bodies rising from the grave to ambush him; in midnight wanderings searching for nothing he would ever find—and the thought of climbing right up to the edge of the bridge, over the motor lanes and across the suspension cables, was too much.

Henry took the interns to lunch one afternoon at his favorite neighborhood pub. He regaled them with tales of Hemingway, Faulkner, Stein, Capote, and someone called Andre Breton. He even knew Foucault, who Henry called "Michel." And forget about all the celebrities he knew—like every star in Hollywood or sports since 1950. He'd even had his head smashed in going two full rounds with an older, semi-retired Joe Louis, and the young Henry had lived to write the tale in his debut, "Palooka Joe," the groundbreaking chronicle of the slow, painful demise of the washed-up legend's career, homing in on the twelve-year reigning champ's recourse to a string of small-purse fights in backwater towns. The champ had squandered his modest fortune in decadence. His debts would haunt him several decades to his grave.

Jeremiah clung to each syllable. After lunch he replayed Henry's every word like a recitation of psalms. He imagined himself as an older gentleman telling stories like this about Henry.

Jeremiah felt stiff, horribly self-conscious and awkward through his first month at work. Now the casual atmosphere, his colleagues' approval, and Henry's gentle magnanimous spirit helped him settle in until Jeremiah felt almost comfortable. He could approach and talk to anyone, even Henry, with a measure of confidence.

Still, Jeremiah might never have struck up the nerve to approach Henry as he would without John—a senior editor, twenty-nine, thirty maybe, who was tall and boyishly handsome with a big, round smiling face. One afternoon, when Jeremiah should have been reading slush, he decided to browse through back issues instead, where he stumbled across John's name. The piece had run four years earlier, an excerpt from a novel John never finished.

Jeremiah asked Laura, an assistant editor, how John had managed to get his piece in the journal. Laura answered grinningly that Henry read submissions from staff on occasion, that people asked him to read their work and if he "really liked" something the *Quarterly* might print it. Jeremiah didn't know if she was making fun of him, or John, or Henry, or all three of them at once, but he sensed the correct response was a vaguely complicit, self-effacing smirk. Laura added, now addressing the other interns—who had stopped working, too—that if any of them were to write something they'd like Henry to read, she encouraged them all (her voice was sincere), but first they should show it to John.

Jeremiah asked John one morning outside the brownstone during a cigarette break. John seemed happy to read his work. Jeremiah printed up and handed him two stories he'd written in college the year before. John returned them a week later with praise: Jeremiah's stories were "brisk" and "intriguing." His prose was "confident and precise" and his characters were "darkly complex" and "robustly defined." John had little in the way of criticism. He quibbled with the endings of both stories, which "felt a little too much like endings," whatever that meant. Still, he too encouraged Jeremiah to send his work upstairs.

Which was exactly what he had hoped for. Here was the real opportunity. He'd imagined this moment. He'd even considered dropping a story of his in the bin upstairs under some clever pseudonym. All the hours of wondering, worrying, strategic planning, etc., were unnecessary in the end. There was no need for stealth, discretion. Fate was effortless, and it came quicker than he'd dared to dream.

He caught Henry outside the building one day. Jeremiah had returned from his lunch break as Henry left for his. Jeremiah's heart slammed in his ears. He found it hard to breathe, but he saw how little was required of him now.

"Yes, certainly. Please do," Henry said. "I would love to read your stories."

The spark was lit. Jeremiah would set the world ablaze in brilliant firestorms of passion. Henry's greatness was his kindling.

After two weeks he got nervous. Yes, Henry ran a literary journal of international renown—albeit a small one—and yes, he was constantly on the phone with authors and patrons. But as far as Jeremiah could tell, despite his recreational visits to the office, Henry wasn't much involved with the day-to-day running of things. He'd pop in now and then to ask something. In editorial meetings his vote affirmed or vetoed the consensus. Still, his schedule could not have been as rigorous as it once was. Surely he had the time to read two stories.

Jeremiah sent Henry an email—not, as he wrote, to rush him—only to thank him again for his time and to say, incidentally, that once Henry found a moment to read the stories Jeremiah would be incredibly grateful, grateful beyond the possibility of reward, were he granted the honor of sitting down to discuss his work with Henry.

Jeremiah arrived the next morning for work and Henry was there in the office. He sat at the counter speaking to John and Tracy. "Oh, Jeremiah. There you are," he said, holding up a manila folder. He stood up from the high wooden stool and approached. Jeremiah looked over at John and Tracy, and both looked away.

Henry gave him the folder. "Just take some time and see if you can…well, *absorb* this first. Then we'll talk. Sound good?" Henry shot him a generous smile.

Dear Jeremiah,

Having begun to read your work, I was discouraged—so much at first that I decided to leave it aside for a while to see if some propitious change in mood might not improve my initial assessment. Alas, it has not.

I fear these stories would require an unholy amount of work to be suitable for publication anywhere, let alone in New World Quarterly. *Apart from your prodigious overuse of adjectives, and the pages of tiresome dialogue that seem to lead nowhere, in the end these stories aren't even stories. They are merely episodes: a disgusting Hollywood actor visits India to be kidnapped, tortured and murdered; a homoerotic mountain man goes whitewater kayaking and drowns senselessly…Your characters don't seem to change from beginning to end. Stories are about change. Furthermore, though you describe each scene to the point of suffocation, I could see very little in all you describe.*

What are you trying to show with these "stories"? What, precisely, is your point?

Please don't be discouraged. Keep at it, old friend, by all means. I think the best advice I might impart to you right now would be to settle down—just relax. Don't work so hard to impress. Try writing a bit cooler.

Fondest regards,
Henry Maxwell

They sat upstairs in his office, next to the desk cluttered with stacks of letters and manuscripts. A photograph of a young Henry next to an old Ernest Hemingway hung on the wall above the desk. Jeremiah and Henry faced off in leather reclining chairs. The Monster wore a burgundy V-neck sweater over a collared shirt with a brown bow tie.

Jeremiah had prepared himself to berate Henry. He'd memorized it all the night before in his bed, where he tossed furiously for hours. He imagined calling Henry out on his rudeness, his condescension and antediluvian sensibilities. How could Henry be blind to his error? How could this great man, in the twilight of his career, abandon the avant-garde and succumb to the tyranny of convention? How could he, Henry Maxwell, sell out in his dotage? Jeremiah would demand all this from him, and more—an apology, for starters.

That had been the plan. But faced with Henry in person, all the confidence and venom drained from Jeremiah. Nothing remained but the dead weight of defeat.

"So, Jeremiah, I hope you didn't find my comments too harsh."

"Well, Henry, as a matter of fact…I did appreciate your… honesty."

"Yes, it really is necessary. Otherwise the whole thing becomes a ridiculous charade. Did you have any questions?"

Jeremiah let the silence fill the vacuum Henry's words left.

"Well, maybe a couple."

He opened the manila folder, which held both stories, along with Henry's and John's comments. Beneath the numbing humiliation and swallowed rage, a spark of defiance thawed his tongue.

"First, I'd like to read you some of what you wrote." He read the first part of the letter, checking Henry's face while he emphasized the old bastard's more vicious attacks. Henry betrayed no sign of remorse. "Now, I'd like to read you some of what John wrote about these same stories." He thrust the pages out in front of Henry like evidence, like Henry was so old and obtuse he needed a visual. He read John's comments aloud, accenting each instance of praise.

"Well," said Henry. "There you have John's opinion." He paused emphatically. "And there you have mine."

"I get it," Jeremiah said. "I'm just having trouble, you know, reconciling these different opinions, since one is so categorically…positive and the other is, well…*not*. Are you suggesting I should ignore what John has to say?"

"No, you can listen to whomever you chose. I wouldn't dream of telling you how to write. But I couldn't imagine what John found praiseworthy in these."

"He isn't the first, you know. This first story won an award when I was in college. T.H. Huffingpough judged the contest, and I think he was shortlisted for last year's National Book Award. And my writing professor at Johnston, Steve Jones? You know him, right?"

"I know and admire him."

"Well, he took me through the revision process on these stories. He signed off on all the changes."

In truth, Jeremiah had spent the last part of the summer reworking the stories, since he couldn't write anything new.

"Why do all of these people, who you know and admire, like these stories?"

"I couldn't imagine."

The conversation continued in this fashion. Neither gave the least ground.

"Look here, now," Henry said. He pulled the manuscript from Jeremiah's hand. "Let's go over these, then, shall we? Let's have a look at what you've written. I wasn't convinced, so here. Convince me. You've certainly convinced John."

Henry read the stories aloud line by line, finding fault with most and saying nothing of the rest. Jeremiah defended every word. That was how they left it an hour later. What cruel trick of fate was this? Why build up his hopes for this bilious old tyrant to shatter?

A few nights later Henry hosted a Christmas party. Jeremiah sat on the couch in the parlor smoking cigarettes with Nina and Pablo. Vonnegut and Mailer were limping around somewhere. A fattish, fiftyish actor he'd seen in a movie or two stood guard over the cheese and vegetable spread on the covered pool table, scanning the room as though to see if anyone recognized him. On the far wing of the parlor a concert pianist friend of Henry's played a sad Greensleeves to a somber crowd.

Half the conversations he heard were about Bin Laden, the rest about Bush—had he known, and what, and when, and what would Bush do next, like all that ever was or would become was somehow tied to one man. Jeremiah resented the idiot, just like everyone else. He read the acerbic columns of Maureen Dowd and Lewis Lapham (the latter smoked beside the Steinway), which Jeremiah felt compelled to wave in the face of his father, who was no lover of Bush, certainly, but believed the proper response to 9/11 would have been to "nuke the whole region."

Which was preposterous, of course. But when Bush bombed Afghanistan Jeremiah had felt better, safer almost. A voice in him that he tried to ignore hoped it would not end there.

He helped tidy up with the rest of the *Quarterly* staff while the guests percolated through Henry's door, downstairs, and out into the cold winter air. Fewer than a dozen heads were left including staff when Henry pulled the tablecloth from the Brunswick and said, "All right. Who's game?" John and Pablo volunteered. Henry looked around. "Jeremiah. Let's go, old friend."

Henry lined up the six in the side corner.

"I was having dinner the other night at Elaine's with my friend, Tim Hutton," he was saying, "and his friend, a TV executive from Los Angeles—Schlitz, I think his name was. Something like that. But the fellow wanted to know if I'd consider doing a number of filmed interviews with celebrities and hosting— or *narrating*, I suppose—a series of biographies for the A&E Network. Smarter than the sort they normally do, I think. Better produced and more interesting, or at least one hopes— nothing on Prince Charles or that sort of thing. I suppose it would be actors, artists, and business entrepreneurs—creative visionary types." Henry sunk his shot. The cue ball stuck on the felt in place of the six.

"Wow, Henry, that's exciting," said John.

"You should totally work that, Henry," Pablo concurred. "I'd be all over that job, even if I had to interview Prince Charles."

"Do you think so, Carlos?" said Henry.

Pablo smiled for John and Jeremiah.

"Absolutely, Henry," Jeremiah said. "Do the show." Then he said, "I think you owe it to posterity."

Henry tucked his cue beneath his arm, reached over, and wrapped Jeremiah in a quick headlock. He knocked his head with his knuckles and then pushed Jeremiah away. The room laughed.

The four of them played on as the others watched. Jeremiah had wanted to play against Henry; Henry insisted they team up. Jeremiah wanted him to fuck up anyway. He'd rather Henry miss so Jeremiah could step up and rescue the pair from defeat. Instead he watched bitterly as Henry sank shot after shot. After a game-winning nine ball off the side post that dropped in the corner, Henry turned to him.

"Did you see that?" he said.

He had seen it all. "Yes, Henry. Nice shot."

Henry pursed his lips in a "come now, let's be friends" expression. The rubber handle of his cue was planted on the floor. He kicked it up and flipped it smoothly to his other palm. Then Henry smiled down at him from his imposing height.

"This takes *years*, Jeremiah. Years."

He carried a flashlight, matches, and seven gallons of gasoline. He used the keys they gave the interns to open the office door. Carefully, he closed it behind him and switched on his flashlight (it never occurred to him that a flashlight beam dancing through the office at one a.m. might look suspicious, too) and lit up the walls of black-and-white photos of Henry schmoozing with celebs. The halo settled on the old brown fixed-gear bike that hung inverted from the ceiling over the basement stairs. The bike was Henry's.

He tiptoed across the room, hoisting the plastic canister to his shoulder; his feet played the dull metal notes of the spiral stairs to the vault where they kept his kind, the wage-less Moorlocks, from the light of day—that dark dungeon that locked in the smell of whatever died in its walls.

He lit up the computers and shelves on the way to the storage room in back. Here it was safe to switch on the overhead light, since the back room had no windows. He unscrewed the cap to the canister spout, and without thinking (he had to remember not to think) he doused the boxes that comprised the *Quarterly*'s archive of back issues, all fifty years.

With half the canister to spare he walked backward through the basement spilling a trail. Reaching the stairs, he searched his pocket for the matches. A shudder of rage and self-disgust— he'd left them in his other coat. He placed the canister on the counter next to the Mac and PC monitors, then crept back up the stairs to the kitchen nook. Luckily, he found some matches near the sink.

The slow descent back to the basement gave him time to think. He'd rather not kill anyone, he thought, but it wasn't impossible. Henry lived upstairs on the second floor, with his much younger wife and two boys. But the fire would start in the basement, and no one lived on the first floor. Everyone upstairs would have time to evacuate. The alarm and sprinklers would go off; the fire department would get the alert, and with any luck they'd extinguish the blaze before it spread higher. And anyway, that fancy antique shit was always insured. It was like in *Trading Places*, when Eddie Murphy started breaking vases and things, and Randolph, the old racist tycoon—who had over-insured everything—got all excited.

He struck the first match and the flame struggled and died stillborn. Smoke wisps curled in the flashlight beam. He shut the flashlight off and put it down to free both hands. Another match failed to light, then another, then one more. He took a breath and drew another match. They were old, stubborn things. By the force of his will they would work.

Again he struck and something surged in him as the flame blossomed in the dark. The glow spread through the room and painted the walls with shadows. The power in that solitary match was overwhelming.

Jeremiah scanned the room in the dim matchlight like a prisoner freed. He stole a last look at his cell before he escaped.

Jeremiah never poured gasoline on the office. He loved to imagine it, though, standing in the dark basement at night. He really had gone down there after the party. He did it to prove how easy it would be, he guessed, or because he hated his room and he hated to sleep and he had nowhere else.

In his months at the *Quarterly* Jeremiah had only browsed a handful of back issues. He'd read none of the very earliest, so he grabbed a few from the shelves and the boxes in back to borrow forever. He found interviews with Borges and Beckett, fiction by Bowles, Marquez, and Roth, and finally Issue 13 (Fall 1958), with Hemingway's interview. The now-famous interview near the end of the giant's life had helped launch the fledgling journal into literary orbit.

Jeremiah got home in the dark hours of the morning. He dropped his bag in his room, skipped brushing his teeth, and took Issue 13 to bed. Like most of the early interviews, Henry conducted Hemingway's personally. But if Henry was the conductor, Hemingway, or "Papa," as Henry called him, was the composer, the creator whose genius and reputation filled the room, and which Henry could only admire, respect, and suffer. So Jeremiah was surprised to read the young upstart Henry stick it to Papa with some tough questions. Papa handled it all as well as he handled anything: he cursed Henry, challenged him to write a better book and stormed from the room in a nuclear burst of vanity. Papa had won the Nobel Prize a few years earlier. Three years later he blew his brains out in Ketchum, Idaho.

For George

INTERLUDE 1

We look at the world once, in childhood.
The rest is memory.
Louise Glück, "Nostos"

Jeremiah *was* scared of his room, but most nights he could sleep safe under his blanket. Tonight, like other nights, he'd cracked the door, closed the closet, left the goose lamp lit; like other nights he'd climbed in bed and hid his face in the crack between the bed and the wall and, for protection, he'd pulled the blanket over his head—but tonight he couldn't sleep.

Still, safe enough in his soft magic shield, he forgot the evil in the room—black shadows in the dark—and he thought about God. At school, he'd learned about God and the place people went when they died, like Moses in the desert. But since he went to a Jewish school, they didn't talk much about Heaven. He'd learned that angels carried Moses up to the clouds. That was it. His first-grade Jewish Studies teacher skipped ahead to Joshua, who led the Israelites to the Promised Land that Moses, so angry and sad to die, wanted so much more than the world in the clouds where God sent him.

Jeremiah stopped her to ask. She told him Jews didn't talk about Heaven. When he asked why not, she looked a little mad and said, "Because you're not supposed to think about it."

He knew he had done something wrong (he always got in trouble at school for behaving bad: staring into space, speaking out in class, and standing on chairs and things) so he asked nothing else. He wasn't supposed to talk about it but he couldn't help imagining—dying, living forever up in a cold white world in the clouds. A hundred years. A *thousand.*

His dad said Heaven was make-believe. When you died you went in the ground and you stayed *there* forever. It would be okay, his father said. He wouldn't miss being alive. To miss something you had to be able think, to feel. When you died, you thought and you felt nothing since your body was dead and your brain died, too.

His father did not believe in God. When Jeremiah asked him why, his dad said if there was a God, He would help his dad's mother, Grandma Ester, who was the most generous person who ever lived and always took care of everyone. That made Jeremiah think.

But he couldn't imagine not thinking at all. He knew what his dad meant, he just couldn't imagine. He could only imagine lying underground in a box, seeing nothing but dark, trying to get out but your arms and legs didn't work. Jeremiah tested his own against the blanket.

He was sleepy now, but even as he sunk down deeper his head kept whispering. What was the thing you looked forward to up in the clouds? If you knew you'd never go anywhere else, would you just sit playing the harp, eating cotton candy like angels in movies and dead cartoons? Would you miss life on Earth? Could you visit?

If not, you could live up there for a thousand years. After a thousand years you must get tired of things. You must get really bored, and not just bored of certain things. After so much time you must get tired of just living. Thinking about all six of the years he'd been alive (each one felt really long), then adding another thousand of those, was too much to think about. That's when the cold hand pushed on his chest and another grabbed his jaw.

He sat up, tossed off the blanket. Had he fallen asleep all the way? Before—was he dreaming? His heart beat loud in his head, really fast at first, then slower until it wasn't so loud anymore and he lay back down and covered up again.

He wasn't supposed to think about Heaven. He didn't like thinking about it, but he hated thinking about no Heaven at all. Imagining living forever in a cold and boring place was better than nothing. What was nothing like? How could he imagine it? He tried hard not to think, but still he thought about thinking nothing.

Jeremiah thought about the time before he was born. He knew the world had been there for millions of years without him. He'd learned about dinosaurs and cavemen, Adam, Abraham, and Moses, about slavery in Egypt and something called "the Holocaust" where bad Germans killed lots of Jews. He knew about these things but he couldn't remember them.

For millions of years he could not see or hear the world. How could you remember something unless you were there to see it? He'd felt nothing. He *was* nothing. That's how it was, then. The world would keep going after he died like it went before he was born, and just like before, he wouldn't be there to remember. He would be nothing again, and only something could remember.

He never worried about what he was before when he was nothing. But he worried now. He worried now that he was something. He wanted to stay that way.

Now his blanket wasn't safe—too hard to breathe, too dark. He threw it off and found the grey ghost of the closet door (he knew whatever was in there was horrible, much meaner, scarier than the little boy's closet monster from the book) and the dim yellow glare of the goose lamp watching him—angry. His throat turned sore. His face grew wet and he stuffed some blanket in his mouth. *I don't wanna live forever*, he said in his head. *I don't wanna die.*

He said it again and again, silently at first and then aloud until the words became a lullaby. Once he relaxed Jeremiah could think of something better.

CHAPTER THREE
Insurrection

We were at some resort in the Latin tropics. I was kicking back on the beach at night in one of those chairs with rubber strips. The rubber stretched against the weight of my large adolescent ass while I drank a Red Stripe and refined my new talent for smoking cigarettes. The other teenagers on the beach that night were boys mostly, from places like Argentina, Italy, and France, and two Portuguese sisters—the older fifteen, the other two years younger—brown and supple in matching white bikinis I couldn't believe their parents let them wear. But they *had*, even earlier in broad daylight.

I'd seen the fifteen-year-old with an older guy. He had a moustache. A big round gut spilled over his black Speedo. They were holding hands, she was smiling, and as they walked past the pool area the man hung back half a step to eye this fifteen-year-old girl and pat her perfect, virtually bare ass. Which seemed pretty sleazy. Then I saw them again the next day at lunch with the younger sister, a brother or two, and their mother. Discovering he was their father made everything worse. Someone said it was a Latin thing.

But that night on the beach I loved them, and saw them in the purest light. I loved both sisters from afar, from a distance too vast to contemplate (try to imagine the distance between two galaxies).

I'd never speak to them, of course, not in six million years. Across the infinite expanse my words would drift and vanish in the void. I could never hope to reach them—not possibly. Why try?

And yet I loved them without words. I loved them only as one who is strangely, tragically compelled to find love everywhere. I imagined my courtships, engagements, marriages, and all variety of intimate exchanges with each sister. I imagined myself with one, the next, and both together.

In real life they spilled their beers and ran in mock distress from slender foreign boys, both sisters in those suits that left so little and so much to imagine. The fronts were three small triangles like sailboats in rough waters; behind they tapered to thin white strings. The ache started somewhere deep, deep down, but seemed to rise and converge in my teeth. I'd never even kissed a girl. I'd just turned seventeen.

My younger sister, Rachel, shared a chair with Antony, a sixteen-year-old French pretty boy. Their audible grappling of tongues was disgusting, as one would imagine. But once, maybe twice, I caught myself watching.

Two hours later the party was dead. My sister and I were left on the beach alone with a lisping, curly-haired Chilean. Alejandro didn't speak English so much as reinvent it. A brave loquaciousness bolstered the limitations of his vocabulary; his sentence constructions were unique. He employed his favorite declarative—"Sox-cer Football est my *live!*"—often and with authority.

Alejandro and my sister, with one year of high school Spanish (she'd switched from French the year before to learn a "language of the people"), managed to communicate well enough to meet somewhere halfway. They'd developed a camaraderie based on Rachel's passion for all things un-American—all things other— and Alejandro's passion for all young American girls.

And yes, she flirted with him. She gave him little hugs and slaps on the shoulder, even sat on his lap once or twice. But Rachel would not make out with Alejandro. She had found her love for this vacation. And even though Antony, heeding his curfew, had stumbled back to his room an hour before;

even though he would leave for France the next morning, and Rachel would never see him again, tonight she would honor his memory.

We drifted and swayed along the beach toward our cabanas. Alejandro stumbled ahead a few paces.

"*An*-to-nee, fuck *you*!" he yelled. He yelled it again, and again, earning a laugh from Rachel each and every time. Then, with a final "Fuck *you*!" Alejandro slunk off to his room.

Rachel and I walked the last stretch of beach toward the far cabanas. Palms hissed in the breeze. Coconuts dropped, smacked the sand. Rachel didn't know we should have been back in our room by eleven, two hours before. She should have known, since the curfew was always eleven. But she asked, and when she did I pretended to forget. I told her I thought he might have said one (he never said one), and fuck Dad anyway, and he would be asleep.

Normally, I would have lacked the nerve to do what I was doing. My father had this way of making you listen.

But on this vacation I was pissed. It was never any one thing, so much as everything about him that pissed me off. I got pissed when he chewed with his mouth open despite all the lectures on dining etiquette he loved to give. I could imagine no worse hypocrisy.

He pissed me off just walking sometimes, ambling like the village idiot with his eyes on the ground and both hands in his pockets. He really, really pissed me off when he failed to notice a fleck of spinach or a glob of salad dressing in the vacation scruff at the corner of his mouth, and he'd keep talking, telling some stupid story for the tenth time and changing the details again. In the past I'd suffered these rages silently. Now they chafed at me like insults. It was all I could do to keep my mouth shut.

More than anything I hated our stupid curfew. I despised the thought of entering my senior year with that mark of shame. It was the same back home, though it wasn't like I had anywhere to be past eleven. The few friends I had were not the kind who drove BMWs and partied till dawn blowing lines in

VIP lounges. Still, I resented knowing kids my age were allowed to do these things and I was not.

I stopped on the beach for one last smoke. We sat and watched the water walls approach, collapse and recede down pebbled slopes. Small crabs left tiny footprints in wet sand. I looked for baby turtle tracks but they'd all disappeared in the tide.

One of the FPs ("Fun Providers") on the resort staff led a beach tour for all new arrivals. My family had taken the tour the morning after we arrived. We learned that turtles dig nests in the sand and guard the eggs they lay. When they hatch, the newborns set out alone (a turtle's role as parent carried fewer expectations). They stumble, awkward and unpracticed in their movements, dragging delicate bodies in brittle shells from sand to surf.

Some never got to swim. From above they were watched, stunned by hurricane-force wings and crushed with talons.

We were eleven minutes late. Though first mandated for eleven, the curfew had been renegotiated and extended to one sometime during dinner, I'd submit. Our mother was sitting up in bed alone. Our father was worried. He'd gone out to look.

"*What*?" I said. "We're only eleven minutes late."

Rachel and I walked back along the beach. We did not speak. I was much colder now. The wind bent the hair on my arms. I told myself it wouldn't be so bad. When we found him he'd probably just get up in our faces. We'd smell his breath while he barked. At most he'd jab a finger in my gut. I'd take it, of course. I'd stand there and wince and imagine snapping it—ripping it off.

That's when I saw him. We stopped. He shuffled toward us looking down. His hands rested in their trusty pockets.

I could taste the salt and seaweed in the air. The waves were louder now. I felt my heartbeat in my eyes, toes, and fingers.

"You're late," he said.

"Only *nine* minutes," I said. My tone surprised me, though as soon as I heard myself I forgot my rebellion. The twenty pounds I had on him meant nothing. I stood still as he rushed us and Rachel screamed.

I hit the sand sideways and he landed on top. One of his hands grabbed my head and my hair mopped the sand. He shouted something I didn't hear. I rolled to my stomach, pushed up on my arms and knees.

Mounted on my back, he rose with me. His knees ground down behind my knees; his arms pulled at mine. Thick arms, thick legs—my body an arc of fat thick steel.

"Get the fuck off me," I said.

I only had to say it once. We held still.

"I'm going to kill you, Jeremiah" he said. Instead he let go.

He may have won the fight until then. He might have kept on winning; it made no difference. The moment he stopped, the contest of wills was lost.

His found an easier test in my little sister.

I stood up and watched as he threw her to the sand. He didn't have to tackle her, just pushed her down and pushed her two more times when she tried to get up. His punishment had lost its edge. Most of his rage was spent on me but he had to do something to even it up. Or maybe to prove he was right the first time, he did it again.

I wouldn't say I was calm, but steady, fluid and alert. I stood outside myself in a power newly earned. And not just earned— *wrested*, like the spoils of years of hard-fought resistance. The insurrection had won its first battle. The taste of long-deferred victory seemed to thrust me closer to the man I would become. Someday I'd be not only angry, but scary too. I'd be no one to fuck with.

Just then I felt how I thought my braver, better self might feel someday, and the special feeling stayed with me as I watched my sister fall, stand halfway and fall again. I could have pushed him away from her. It even crossed my mind. I might have been scared. Maybe my new bravery was a fluke, some short-lived mutation of personality. Or maybe I thought she deserved what she got as much as I did.

A year before that he and I were in the driveway playing basketball at our country house upstate. We were playing 21, disagreeing over some rule in relation to one of his shots. I kept arguing until he tossed the ball over his shoulder into the grass, then walked off toward the house and said he didn't want to play with a jerk.

"Don't call me a jerk," I said. "Asshole."

He turned, and almost before I could blink he had closed the distance between us, grabbed my thick, flabby arms and pushed me backward up the driveway. He let go and shoved me again.

"Come on, *big boy*," he dared. But I just stood there. My mom was in the house somewhere.

Afterward he took me out on the guesthouse porch, far from the house and everyone so we—or he—could talk. He never, ever would have called his father an asshole, no matter how pissed he was at him. The relationship commanded a certain respect. Certain lines should never be crossed. His lesson reminded me of a social studies class in elementary school on the Greeks. Mr. Steve, my sixth-grade teacher, talked about the wisdom of the ancients—the moral philosophy of our Western forefathers. We learned about their passion for democracy, their fear and distrust for their gods, and the common belief that any father had the right to kill a son who disobeyed him.

When my father talked about his dad, the man he'd named me for, I felt the familiar conflict of reverence and shame. This was my father's father, the paragon of a man I'd never met. For me he existed only in my dad's legends: Grandpa Joe, the college football star, one of the first and only Jews to play in the NFL; the Air Corps major and bombardier with two bronze stars from WWII; the man's man, the man-to-end-all-men whose flaws seemed only to brighten his star. Like his year-long suspension from the University of Wisconsin, where he was caught with a naked woman—his forty-year-old high school vice principal—in his room at proscribed hours.

Then there was his legendary smoking habit—four packs a day. He'd wake up every morning at five, or four thirty, to light his first. Once my father asked him why he woke up so early. So he could smoke more, was the answer.

Had I listened to the silences between my father's words, entombing his father like the golden sarcophagus of an Egyptian king; had I read the legend's subtext, I may have thought more about smoking. What was the void he filled each day with the smoke and tar of eighty cigarettes? Was it something to do with the war? Was it the reform school my grandfather's immigrant parents sent him to as a boy, where Franciscan monks thrashed the demons out of the little Jew so he would do his best to beat them out of my dad, and so on? Was it something no one knew about, something my grandfather never discussed?

The only weakness I felt when my dad talked about his was mine by comparison to this god among men, who was somehow meant to survive in the first letter of my name. I said nothing, just sat there and listened as hatred for my father turned to shame, and shame to sadness the more he talked about his dad, then his mother, who'd died of Alzheimer's when I was twelve. Whatever point he intended to make was lost, and the sermon became an excuse, any excuse to remember and talk about his parents. I watched his face and his words assume a softer tone. I knew him then. He was the loneliest man alive.

Rachel and I slept through breakfast. We woke up just in time for lunch. My parents, my sisters, and I ate with a couple from the Upper West Side, like us, whom my parents had met on the beach the day before. The sisters from Portugal sat with their parents across the patio. Towels covered their asses while they ate, though they wore the same skimpy white tops. I leered at them between bites, but my heart wasn't in it today.

Slowly and without pleasure I ate every scrap of eggs, beans, and sausage heaped on my plate, then piled on the sickly sweet mango, the kiwi and pineapple slices and cubes of cheese. I ate with unusual focus, tracing the mashed-up clots down my throat to my gut. After each bite I felt fatter.

Rachel and I said nothing. She sat looking down at her wasted plate of cheese and fruit. Our parents chatted up their new vacation pals, the people on this particular trip who they'd exchange numbers with and pretend they would see again. In two, three years one of them would say, "Remember that nice couple? The Kornsteins, at Punta Brava?"

Then they'd remember the cabanas, the turtles, the breakfast patio and the Family Variety Show Extravaganza Dinner Gala on the last Saturday. Someone would recall how friendly and attentive the resort staff was, how hard they worked to motivate the guests, to get us all involved and make sure everyone had fun.

He pulled me aside after lunch. He thought we might discuss the night before. Birds cackled in the palms. Screams came from the pool. I faced him obliquely.

"I thought we discussed it," I said.

The night before, he took us back to our room and yelled at us for thirty more minutes. He'd been searching for over an hour. He'd decided we had left the gated resort and gone to the local bar, where someone must have slit our throats. It happened all the time in Third World countries. Rachel and I sat on the bed, and I stared him dead in the eye while he paced the room and avoided mine.

"That was me yelling, not a discussion."

I said nothing. The screams from the pool got louder. They sounded more heartfelt than before. Then I saw the thick dark cloud in the water.

The same thing happened the day before. The resort put a chemical in the pool to alert the guests whenever some brat pissed his Speedo. Now it would be evacuated, drained, and refilled.

My father turned from the pool to face me again. The day was bright and clear. I could see the deep furrows of his brow and the lines cascading from his eyes.

"You wouldn't want a father who didn't care," he said. "They're worse."

And maybe that was true, but looking back I think he meant I wouldn't want a father who was dead.

CHAPTER FOUR
How Code Works with Science

|

The emperor's legions attacked from below in a massive coordinated assault. Jeremiah planned and led the attack, and the victory bore the signature of his evil genius. It ended with Jeremiah unleashing a river of fire from his chest and fingertips up on the great white cloud where God mounted His futile defense. The shock and awe of Jeremiah's hellfire beams proved too fierce for the Almighty, who retreated to higher clouds to hide and recoup.

Jeremiah chose to let Him go. He would risk a fight with God another day. He preferred to let Him live.

But the gates of Hell hung open now. The Dark Emperor, Lord Jeremiah, and their minions could leave by day to pillage and conquer, then retire below for a night of romance with the Dark Lady Samantha, Vice Queen of the Underworld. Jeremiah could see her when he closed his eyes: her black negligee, her violet high boots and matching lipstick, her tight black-leather bodice. Samantha dressed a lot like Evil-Lyn, Skeletor's lusty courtesan. Lord Jeremiah had long black horns, and a long black cape, and all kinds of weapons popped from a hatch in his scalp like the bad guy in *Time Bandits*.

This was the kind of dream Jeremiah had when he was awake—the kind he controlled. He would dream in the shower; on the toilet; on the bus to school. He dreamed through class, on the bus, and at home when he sat in his room at his desk to "work." Jeremiah loved to dream anytime but when he should have been—when he was asleep. Those dreams were bad. He didn't like to remember them. So maybe he had to make up for it during the day with dreams he liked.

It hardly mattered at first. For a few weeks he fooled everyone, as usual. He fooled his parents, his babysitters, even Miss Eisenreich.

Jeremiah had been scared to have Miss Eisenreich since at least third grade. The shrill cries of her discipline sometimes carried all the way across the hall to Mrs. Goldman's room. He loved Mrs. Goldman, who liked him too, and liked children. He had Mrs. Goldman two years straight. The summer before fifth grade darkened with impending change.

But things would be different this year, he told himself. He would rise to the dreaded occasion. Jeremiah would learn to motivate himself without the extra patience and attention he knew were conditioned upon Mrs. Goldstein's affection for him, which had saved him for two years. This year, he would slay the beast with emergency secret reserves of discipline and good behavior. He would work, he would stay out of trouble and win Miss Eisenreich's heart, too. He would find her soft spot, charm her as he had charmed Mrs. Goldman. Miss Eisenreich's strictness, her temper would keep him in check and finally unlock the hidden "potential" his father insisted Jeremiah had. He insisted over and over, until the elusive gifts Jeremiah was meant to possess took on the emotional correspondence of guilt. Talk of his potential evoked a burden that seemed to grow with the endless accumulating and disappearing of days when Jeremiah could have learned something but he chose to waste them instead, dreaming.

II
[The Fifth Reich]

Miss Eisenreich's first coup was changing all their seats.

For two years his class had sat in seats of their own choosing.

Mrs. Goldman let them choose their seats so long as no one asked to change (she wasn't a babysitter, and this wasn't musical chairs). And that was fine because people mostly kept the same friends they'd started with in third grade. The one adjustment that would be necessary going into fifth was that Brandy and Samantha, being new best friends, would need to sit together. Jeremiah would have to sit there, too.

But Miss Eisenreich devised her own final solution. History would reveal that her actions were calculated, and carried out with a cold, mechanical precision. It was all mapped out in a seating chart designed to maximize their pain, which she dropped on them like a hydrogen bomb the very first day of class.

"This is so *unfair!*" cried Brandy Bloom. She ran from the room.

"Bray-ann-dy!" shrilled Miss Eisenreich with the riot horn she wielded for a voice.

Samantha slumped despondently. She lingered across from Jeremiah in the seat she would have to abandon for another at the next table, right next to Shayna Schatz.

Jeremiah was sad, too. But he said nothing. It was too soon for defiance. Without argument, he gathered his books and supplies and took his new seat in the corner of the grey trapezoid up front between Avi and Richard.

"But Miss Eisenreich," said Samantha, "it's just that we're used to our old seats. We've sat with our friends for two years now." She still hadn't moved. Miss Eisenreich would not know that Samantha and Brandy had not sat together those two years.

Miss Eisenreich's head rose. "This isn't playtime, Samantha," she said. "This is the fifth grade, and you are all here to learn."

Her next atrocity consisting in assigning them homework like they'd never had. Mrs. Goldman never assigned half as much.

And as though she hadn't yet bled them of enough freedom and dignity, Miss Eisenreich also banned all talking during Thursday "study hall." Mrs. Goldman would let them talk quietly.

"That was fourth grade," she would say, like fourth grade had been some paradise like the Garden of Eden, but somehow they blew it and now they were screwed. "This is fifth."

Jeremiah sought to avoid confrontation with Miss Eisenreich. In the early weeks he succeeded. When she yelled, she yelled at other kids mostly—like Horace Bello, who couldn't sit still or stay quiet even for a minute, and couldn't help getting in trouble. Jeremiah felt bad for Horace.

She did scold Jeremiah once or twice, like when she caught him drawing cartoons in math. At least she never caught him drawing her, which he often did—her mousy brown curls flared like a nest, her square black glasses doubled in size and thickness with bulgy, solid-black holes for eyes. Sometimes he even drew her farting, with streaks of lead or blue ink streaming from the skirt of the shapeless blue dress with little white flowers she wore all the time. (If she found those, he thought, he would be expelled.)

She started writing comments on his homework, too ("sloppy…incomplete…this is all wrong…"), but things were okay. The situation, though far from ideal, was under control.

III

Everything changed about six weeks in, the night his mother and father came home from the first parent-teacher conference. Jeremiah had spent several days pretending Miss Eisenreich would have only good things to report. That night he preferred not to think about it.

Instead he sat at his desk and plotted his own coup in Hell. He was sick of the Dark Emperor and tired of playing second fiddle. Jeremiah was strong enough to rule. The Dark Lady Samantha caressed and encouraged him, feeding his ambition in the dark lair—the Imperial Chamber ten thousand miles below the earth. Then she started undressing.

In real life they never once kissed. They were only ten, and Jeremiah wasn't sure he'd even want to kiss Samantha, or anyone for real yet. He wasn't even sure how Samantha was his "girlfriend," except that everyone knew she was, and that was important.

She had been his date for the square dance at the three-day orientation at Brambles Park and Nature Reserve in the South Jersey woods. Jeremiah's class at Havarim Tovim Elementary School on the Upper West Side went to Brambles each year before school, grades four to six. After the adventure walks, the cooperation games, and the ruminations on the year ahead corralled in cross-legged circles by lake and campfire—after two days of activities that he and his friends mocked constantly but really enjoyed, they gathered for the dance in the grand ballroom. (Brambles called it "The Wreck Lodge," which was totally stupid, he thought, and made no sense.)

Jeremiah's date the year before was Brandy Bloom. She'd been his girlfriend in third grade. She was Jason Sweinberg's girlfriend, too, he guessed, but at the end of the year she told Jeremiah she loved him more than Jason. Either way, it was she who'd started calling herself their girlfriend, which meant they each had lots of playdates with her playing Super Mario Brothers for hours.

By the next year she would love them no more. She told him at the fourth grade dance. Brandy, with her ripped stonewash jeans and big dark eyes, became, officially, the most popular girl in their class of twenty-one that year, and that was the year when things like that really started to matter. Soon she started loving his friend, Ben, an athletic blond—already pushing five foot five—even though he hardly spoke to her or any girls.

Jeremiah was devastated. His nightly, sometimes tearful prayers did nothing to win her back, which upset him, and it upset him even more to be upset with God.

On playdates with Jason, Jeremiah said nasty things about Ben. He got Jason to say stuff, too. They hated him, they agreed more than once, and talked about kicking his ass, though at school they were all still friends and no one said anything. But the whole year he daydreamed of fighting Ben for Brandy, smashing his nose with a flying jump kick that Jeremiah knew— even though every Saturday he took karate at the Y—he could never pull off. He wouldn't want to since Ben was his friend.

He daydreamed about Brandy, too. He dreamt of being older with her, of walking down the street with her alone and holding hands. He imagined driving in red Ferraris and Corvettes with her sitting next to him, her long black hair flaring out in the wind, "I Need a Hero" blasting on the stereo. In arts and crafts he drew them together in the sporty red convertibles, always relishing in the nuances of composition: the yellow-marker dots of headlights; the streaking pencil lines behind the car evoking the inferno thrust of speed; the thin black-marker sunglasses they always wore in his drawings, though never in life. Unschooled in the formal techniques of perspective, Jeremiah could not draw her beside him up front (she always sat behind, in back).

When the class sat on the floor of the gym and Pat, their gym teacher, talked, Jeremiah imagined the thick steel cord of a huge light fixture hanging from the high ceiling snapping loose right above where Brandy sat. He would spring up and tackle her out of the way, like he'd seen on *The Brady Bunch*, before the deafening crash of metal and glass (hopefully it would miss whoever sat nearby). She would have to love him then, or basically. He always tried to sit close to her—though never *too* close—just in case.

Nothing like that ever happened, though. No thanks to God.

But now Jeremiah's prayers had been answered finally, albeit the next-best answer. At first there was just Jennifer Goldstein. He had asked Jenny to the dance before school ended the year before that (the uncertainty of a summer with no date for the dance would have been too much). Then, on the bus to Brambles, Jeremiah learned that over the summer Brandy had become good friends with Samantha. Samantha wasn't as pretty as Brandy. That said, she was blonde. Furthermore, her new allegiance with Brandy conferred on Samantha the clear distinction of second-most-popular girl. So Brandy convinced him to trade Jennifer Goldstein—who was pretty, but not so popular—for Samantha, who didn't want to go with Jason, who hadn't been as fat the year before when he'd asked her. Samantha said yes to Jeremiah, who dumped Jennifer, who got stuck with fat Jason Sweinberg after Samantha dumped him.

Jeremiah and Samantha were shy at first. They avoided meeting eyes, and clutched awkwardly at each other throughout the square dance led by Brambles staffer Longhorn Bob in his boots and ten-gallon hat, hollering do-si-dos—too shy, the two of them, even to roll their eyes. Jeremiah was very much aware, constantly, of his expanding waist, which was nothing like Jason's but still noticeable, he thought. It had been checked at camp that summer, but grew again in the month at home watching TV and stuffing his face with Double Stuf Oreos.

But when they played the good stuff—Michael Jackson, Huey Lewis and the News, Tiffany, songs they all knew and sang but mostly couldn't understand—and the hollers and fiddles faded to the exotic familiar melodies, they danced more expressively—arms pumping, Jeremiah stomping in place like an eager soldier, Samantha presciently mirroring the slide-sneakered, upper-body thrust that would soon become "The Running Man" to tweens the world over. And by the end, when the great new song the popular girls had been hoping for, which Jeremiah heard that night for the very first time and would never forget—when "Kokomo" played, their tired arms rested on each other's shoulders.

Jeremiah forgot the other dancers—Jennifer and Jason, Jacob Fox and Lindsey Stern, Amy Feld and Jon Burger, and Shlomit and Avi, the Israelis. He forgot the rejects on the side who had stopped the moment the mandatory square-dance portion ended. He forgot Sam Kornfeld and Sarah Weiner, Shayna Schatz and Richard Dweibman. He forgot about Ben, who had gone outside, leaving Brandy alone with the nerds (he had seen her standing there, arms crossed, embarrassed, sullen and confused; did she see him?). And when the song climaxed with the burning saxophone solo and Jeremiah's thumb grazed Samantha's skin between covered shoulder and bare neck, he forgot Brandy Bloom. He forgot the song, the room, and the years before and ahead. In the timeless moment sealed in the crook of a soft, bare neck Jeremiah stood within himself. He *forgot* himself. And God.

He heard the click of the lock in the outside door, through the half-closed door of his bedroom. He dreaded that sound most nights. He pulled out his algebra book, flung it open, slammed it down on the desk, and stared at page ninety-four like he'd been transported, mesmerized by the magical world of numbers and variables.

"Hey, Jair," said his mom. He looked up in mock surprise.

They stood at the entrance to his room. They looked disappointed, though not too upset. They both kissed him goodnight.

"We'll talk about school tomorrow," said his dad. "Get some sleep. There are things to discuss, but it wasn't too bad. You're gonna have to watch yourself with this one, though. Miss Eisenreich is a real shrew."

"Oh, Allen." His mom stared at his dad.

"What?" he said. "You heard her talk to me."

She looked away.

"Who shot that?" said Mrs. Eisenreich. It had actually hit her, and right on the butt. It sent a ripple through the patch of white flowers. His first thought was to be impressed at his own range of fire and accuracy, though he hadn't aimed it really. He was only playing with it stretched around his index finger and thumb when it slipped.

"Oh, sorry," Jeremiah said all nonchalant, like he'd shot his best friend. It never occurred to him to lie. "I wasn't trying to shoot it." It occurred to him only then he might be in serious trouble.

She said nothing else, though. She just turned back around and finished chalking up the board. Then she told the class to find partners for the grammar exercise. "Not you, Jeremiah," she said. "You need to go down to Mr. Schechter's office."

Something in his stomach dropped. "Why?" It came out a whisper.

"To see Mr. Schechter."

"What for?"

"Because," she said, "you *shot* me with a rubber band."

"What? No! I said it was an accident."

"I heard you before. You still need to go."

"But…why?" His eyes grew blurry and wet.

"Jer-e-miah."

"I won't."

"*Jeremiah.*"

"*No!*"

"The thing that consoins me here, Jeremiar, is not this incident. I mean, you say it was an accident, so it was an accident. I believe you."

Jeremiah liked Mr. Schecter, the school principal. He liked his trim sideburns and his bald, shiny head—like Mr. Clean—and he liked how Mr. Schechter talked, even though he called him "Jeremiar." But Jeremiah dreaded being sent to Mr. Schecter's office.

"What consoins me most is a paddin I see developing. And we've seen it before with you, no? Not so much last year with Mrs. Goldman, but what about second grade? Rememba? With Judy Saks?"

Oh, he remembered.

"You're not doing your homework. You're horsin' around in class, drawing pictures when you should be loining math. And this time you were horsin' around, and you shot your teacher in the tush with a rubbaband. You're a smot kid, Jeremiar, but that's not smot."

If he was always doing stupid things, then how was he smart?

"If it were just one thing I might keep this between us. But I don't want you getting off to a bad stot this year. I'll have to cawl your fawtha."

He reached for his rolodex, picked up his phone.

"No!"

Mr. Schechter hesitated. He looked surprised.

"Not my dad, Mr. Schecter! Please! He'll *kill* me!"

Mr. Schecter set the phone back down on the receiver. "Whaddaya talkin' about?"

"He will! I swear to God, he will! Please don't!"

"Jeremiar, your fawtha's not gonna kill you. He's a good man. Your parents love you very much. Whaddaya getting all hysterical—"

"Please!"

"Okay. Okay. All right. Settle down, Jeremiar. I won't cawl him this time. Relax. Okay?"

Jeremiah nodded.

"But you bedda shape up in class. Next time, I cawl."

IV

Jeremiah watched his stomach rise from the bathwater—a sperm whale hump, distended, breaking the surface. It collapsed, dove down with each tense breath.

He eyed the flesh mounds of his thighs and the little fat folds of his chest. Absently he poked and strummed the knob between his legs. He caught himself and stopped, repulsed.

It was one of those moments when Jeremiah became aware of himself. Looking down at himself in the tub, at the body he hid beneath loose t-shirts, Jeremiah grew embarrassed at the thought of someone watching him. He imagined Samantha could see him there, as he was. He was flabby and gross, and he felt her disgust and the sting of her laughter.

Next Jeremiah imagined his fat wet body exposed to the watchful eyes of certain dead relatives. They were among the ghosts who monitored him always. He felt their eyes on him no matter where he was, and, seeing himself, was seldom proud to be seen. He imagined his father's father cringing from above. He pictured his ancestral hero, a man he'd never met, full of shame at the sight of him. Of course he would regret everything Jeremiah was, and all that he could never be. Jeremiah could not blame him.

V

(Dr. Franny)

Dr. Franny was the school psychologist. She was thirty maybe. She wore grey and blue pantsuits with shoulder pads. Jeremiah's parents made him talk to Dr. Franny every Wednesday while the other kids ate lunch. You could eat in her office.

He had to talk to Dr. Franny since he wasn't doing well in school. His first trimester report had not been good. So Dr. Franny tested him, but Jeremiah had a good IQ (his ability to repeat number sequences backward was "off the charts" though he could never tell left from right, which lowered his score and that didn't seem fair), so really there was no excuse for him— none but laziness, which was no excuse at all.

Dr. Franny's job, he guessed, was to figure out why he was such a disappointment to his parents, to his teachers, and most of all—like his dad always said—to himself.

So every Wednesday Dr. Franny sat in a leather reclining chair across from his, where he sat grabbing his knees, or hunched forward with his arms folded to hide his gut. She would ask about school, about home, and lots about Jeremiah's dad. She asked about his job, what time he came home, how much Jeremiah got to see him—stuff like that—and she'd take notes. She asked him things like, "Is it hard for you when you feel that your father is upset with you?" and he always ended up crying.

One Wednesday, after a good, long sob, Dr. Franny switched to a happier topic. She asked about "cliques" at school, whether they existed in his fifth-grade class. Jeremiah said yes, there were certain cliques, separated in terms of "popularity." At the foot of the body politic sat the rejects and nerds. The midsection represented the somewhat popular group, or those students whose status shifted depending on the day or mood. Finally, at the crown of the kingdom, sat the "most popular" kids.

"Which group are you in?" Dr. Franny wanted to know. Her eyes watched him.

"The *most* popular group," he said, wiping the snot from his nose with a soggy tissue.

"*That's* good," she said, and she wrote something down.

Soon the verdict was in. Dr. Franny finished her report on him, which reached him by way of his parents. Attached to a full breakdown of Jeremiah's Intelligence Quotient (it was high, she said, though lowered by his "performance IQ"—more evidence he never met his potential), Dr. Franny typed up a twelve-page diagnosis of Jeremiah, which could be reduced to the following: Jeremiah's dad was a hardworking, successful man—which was hard sometimes—and Jeremiah missed him while his dad worked long hours.

None of which seemed right to Jeremiah, or it didn't explain enough. But Dr. Franny's report seemed to offer excuses for him. He would take it.

VI

[The Camps]

Jeremiah spent every summer at camp. He hated camp.

And not just the ones where he stayed overnight, though they were the worst; the first camp he hated was at the YMCA just three blocks from home.

Most of Jeremiah's friends from school went to Jewish camps, places with names like Yomi or Shlomi. Jeremiah's parents wanted him to get to know other kids besides Jews.

Two summers before, at the Y, he moved from the junior to the senior camper group where, not yet eight -years old, he was the second youngest of twelve campers. And he hated it because:

1. The other campers always laughed at how stupid he was.

2. Everyone teased him for being fat (in camp, unlike school, you had to change and swim in front of other kids).

3. Tim, a thirteen-year-old from Texas, who was six feet tall, taller than both counselors. He bullied Jeremiah the most and riled up the rest against him, threw a half-opened can of Coke at his head, which smacked Jeremiah's face and spilled all over him. He threw it right in front of Pam, the counselor, who punished Tim from Texas with twenty silent minutes in the corner of the room.

4. Jeff, his nineteen-year-old junior counselor, informed Jeremiah once that he, Jeff, "got laid more times in one weekend" than Jeremiah would "in his whole life." Which didn't bother Jeremiah so much, since he was seven and in no rush. But when Jeremiah suggested Jeff's mother didn't count, Jeff grabbed Jeremiah, locked his head, and clubbed him with a broad, blunt elbow.

5. When he told his mom one morning that he hated the Y, and that all the kids hated him and called him names, she frowned at him and said, "Sticks and stones." When he answered that they did hit him sometimes, even the counselor once, she said that wasn't nice, and to tell her if he they did it again. Then she went to work and dropped him off at camp.

Basically he hated it because he had no choice. When he thought about it, it was kind of like jail.

Later that summer he spent his first week at "sleep-away" camp. He'd been looking forward to it for months. It was clearly a rite of passage for boys, and he left determined to embrace the challenge.

The third day in, they were playing soccer when the ball rolled at Jeremiah, and Greg, on the opposite team, rather than kicking the ball away decided to bash Jeremiah's nose with his head.

Jeremiah cried out, but he didn't tear up. He marched toward Greg with one fist raised. Greg's back was turned. He was walking away.

"Hey, Jeremiah! Greg!" yelled Seth, a counselor with a big humped nose and meaty red lips. "Greg, take a seat—for the rest of the game. None of that rough stuff. This is soccer, not football. Understand?"

That was it?

"Jeremiah."

He was still eyeing Greg.

"*Jeremiah.*"

"*What?*"

"Are you okay?"

"I don't know."

"Where does it hurt?"

"My *face.*"

Seth walked over. "Tell me if it hurts." Seth touched his nose.

"*Yes.*"

"Bad?"

"Not *so* bad."

"You're okay. You can keep playing if you want."

The game started back up. Jeremiah hung back near the sidelines with Greg, who sat on the bench. Greg held his head in his hands. Jeremiah watched him, waiting for him to look up. He wouldn't, so Jeremiah looked over at Seth, who was busy watching the game, then turned back to Greg.

"Nigger," he said.

He'd heard it only once, maybe twice. He had no idea what it meant, he just knew it was bad—maybe the worst thing he could say.

"Yo *mutha!*"

"Greg!" Seth yelled.

"He called me a *nigga*!"

Seth turned to Jeremiah. "What?" Seth walked fast at him. "Did you?"

Jeremiah said nothing.

Seth grabbed Jeremiah's arm and pulled him away from the field, crying.

"*Never* use that word. That's a horrible, horrible word." Seth sat face to face with Jeremiah in the small equipment shed. "So what if he's black, and you're white?"

But that wasn't it. He didn't hate black people—just Greg. But he couldn't explain.

"How old are you? Eight?"

"In two weeks I am."

"Okay, so you're eight. Who taught you that word?"

A schoolmate of his, a boy in the grade above Jeremiah had dared him to ask Calvin, their bus driver, what it meant. And he did, but Jeremiah wasn't expecting Calvin would be so mad at him about some word he didn't even know. He didn't yell at Jeremiah, but his voice was angry in a quiet way, and soon Calvin got quiet, too. And he didn't believe that Jeremiah didn't know what it meant. Jeremiah felt bad afterward. He would for years.

"Do you even know what it means?"

Jeremiah shook his head. Seth never explained.

Another counselor hit him that summer, too. It happened on his last full day at Clendaniel. He was in the Shop Shack for arts and crafts, one of his "electives." Frankie, a CIT with bushy black eyebrows and crossed, close-set eyes, led the class (Jeremiah was pretty sure Frankie was at least sort of retarded). Seth was around to supervise. He stepped out for a minute and everyone took advantage. Kids started throwing clay and standing on chairs and Frankie got mad.

"Guys, stop it! Stop it, guys! Now!"

Jeremiah reached across the table for an unopened can of

blue Clay Dough, even though he knew he wasn't allowed to have any more.

"Jeremiah, *no*," Frankie warned.

He picked it up anyway.

"I said STOP!" And Frankie reached across the table and judo-chopped him on his neck from the side with the edge of his palm.

"Frankie!"

Seth was back to check the noise.

"That is *not* okay, Frankie. Come here." Godlike, Seth saw and knew everything.

The two stepped out for a minute. The room was quiet.

Frankie approached him after class. He was crying.

"Jeremiah, I'm really, really sorry," he said. "I was really mad, and I lost my temper, and I'm really, really sorry. Okay?"

"Okay." And he did understand, and he was sorry too, and sad.

Those were just some of the things he would always remember.

VII

Jeremiah kind of liked science. He was okay at it.

He never liked experiments or equations, none of that boring math and lab crap. He hated math and he sucked at it (math was for the Richard Dweibmans of the world), and labs were a pain, though he liked cutting open the frozen frog in a gross kind of way, and the time when Mr. Simon, a bearded Australian Jew—like really from Australia, with the funny accent and everything—the one and only science teacher at Havarim, let everyone drop Alka-Seltzer pills into meniscuses full of water stopped with rubber corks, then watch as they burst sequentially in a twelve-cannon salute, smacking the hollow white tiles on the science room ceiling.

He liked knowing the names of things. Jeremiah knew mountains, oceans, rivers, jungles, planets, and stars. He was good with proportions and distances. He liked to separate things, to compare and parse them out in natural hierarchies, ranking the animals in order of ferocity, speed and intelligence, or the planets by mass, distance from the Earth or the Sun, and how many moons spun in their orbits. He could name the largest stars in the galaxy, and the closest, and brightest.

What he liked most about science, though, was more than knowing everything; he wanted to know how everything started, too—life, the universe, where it was going and how it would end.

Science, he was discovering, had better answers than the Torah.

He heard the same stories about giant fish, talking snakes, ancient floods with rainbow promises, and nine-hundred-seventy-five-year-old men every year, and they only got stupider. His father enjoyed the stupidity of these stories, and sharing the joke with Jeremiah, who saw his dad's point more and more but found it harder to laugh.

Mr. Simon, who wore a kippah, never talked about God except to say that He existed, or he believed in Him at least, and science could not prove him wrong, or not yet, so until it could Mr. Simon would go on believing in "Gode." Which made Jeremiah feel better.

VIII

"Do you care, Jeremiah?" His father had asked the question before.

The second trimester reports were in. Jeremiah got a pretty good report from Hagit, his Hebrew teacher—except for his behavior—and from Nancy for art. Which was nice, except who spoke Hebrew, so who cared? And everyone knew art didn't count.

They only had science on Tuesdays at Havarim, which meant no reports from Mr. Simon. His father called it "scandalous." Jeremiah agreed, since he kind of liked science, and he liked Mr.

Simon a lot, and he guessed he might get a pretty good report from him, which would help right now.

In all other subjects, Miss Eisenreich wrote, Jeremiah's efforts were "haphazard." His failure to finish homework assignments and his "unfocused, disruptive" behavior in class were the old handwritten, stapled, pink-slipped composition's themes. The familiar two-pronged assault was delivered aloud in his father's hard voice. His voice and hers went at him together, but he heard the words so often they struck like obsolete munitions. The odd word, a special turn of phrase stung now and then, but the ground had hardened.

They sat in his parents' bedroom. His father leaned forward from his seat at the edge of the bed. Jeremiah slouched back in his dad's desk chair.

"Do you? Do you care about getting into a good high school, or being successful in life? Huh?" His father's finger stabbed the pink report at every question mark. "If you tell me you don't, I'll stop bothering you."

He said this often, too. Jeremiah wondered.

"But if you do care, Jeremiah," and he knew what came next, "then it's my job to push you."

He didn't care—not really, not anymore. The first six million times he cared, and now he wanted to be left alone. Not caring was no real option, though. He held his breath to stop his tears, then tried to hide them.

"So tell me, Jeremiah—*look* at me."

Jeremiah's head jerked up.

"Do you care?"

"*Yes.*"

"Why are you crying?"

He never did know how to answer that.

"You know, Jeremiah, at first when we'd have these talks, and you'd start crying, I used to feel sorry for you. I thought maybe I was a little hard on you sometimes, and I'd feel bad. But how many times have we had this conversation?"

Once more and Jeremiah could stab him in the throat.

"And you know it's not because you're not smart. You read Dr. Franny's report. You're very smart. And you can do well when you try. Like last year with Mrs. Goldman. Right?"

Jeremiah nodded.

"But this year you got lazy. You say your homework is done when I come home, but all I see is a half-empty box of cookies, and you sitting on your big ass playing that fucking Nintendo."

What did he expect him to do? Go for a jog in the park?

"Do you think Super Mario Brothers is gonna come up on the ERBs?"

If only.

"Why is everything such a distraction for you? Why can't you concentrate?"

Maybe he should go to concentration camp.

"That Miss Eisenreich's a real bitch. I know it. You know it. So what? If you know she's out to screw you, don't give her the chance. Just do your work and she can't do a damn thing. Right?"

"Right."

"So tell me, why should I feel sorry for you? I just start talking, and you start crying. I don't even have to yell at you. I'm not yelling now, am I?

For him, he was not.

"But you cry anyway. And you cry to Mr. Schechter, too, and you say, 'Oh, God, please, Mr. Schechter! Don't tell my father. He'll beat the crap out of me!'" He whirled his hands theatrically. "And you know that's not true. Right?"

He hadn't known Mr. Schechter called. "No." He was embarrassed.

"So why do you say that? And why are you crying now? You know, you cry, and I start thinking maybe I don't need to punish you. Maybe you're disappointed enough in yourself, and you really want to do better. Maybe you want to lose weight so kids won't laugh at you. Maybe they laugh already. They laughed at me when I was your age. I was heavier than you but you're getting there, boy. It's not fun.

"You may think life's tough now, kiddo, but it's gonna get worse. In ten, twenty years, you'll be very unhappy."

Jeremiah believed it.

IX

It was fourth period, the first class after lunch. Jeremiah and his classmates took their marks around the grey tabletops. He heard backpack zippers, the metal teeth of trapper-keeper binders. Waves of chatter rose and fell. Miss Eisenreich took the helm at her desk. She prepared the blackboard for social studies.

Jeremiah was talking to Avi, whom he'd grown to like. He even enjoyed sitting with Avi. Avi sometimes taught Jeremiah how to curse in Hebrew: *Bool bool, Ben Zona, Tzitzim Gadolim*.

Avi's English was improving, too. In third grade, Avi's first year in the States, he could say almost nothing. Now he was telling Jeremiah how to approach an Israeli girl for sex. In Israel, said Avi, when a boy wanted to have sex with a girl he would ask her to "go outside" with him.

Jeremiah was shocked at the thought of Israeli teenagers engaging in casual sex (did that sort of thing really happen there, in the Holy Land?), and his mind fixed on the mystery of what going outside had to do with sex. Then he heard his name intoned in the voice of Brandy Bloom.

"Jeremiah." He craned his neck around. "Samantha has something to tell you."

They sat together behind him at Samantha's table. Shayna Shatz was displaced from her given seat, as usual. Shayna stood in the corner, towering over the fifth-grade class at a freakish five foot six, arms crossed, scowling and waiting for class to start so she could reclaim her place.

Then Samantha said, "I'm dumping you."

"Fine," he said, and turned back around.

He did not resume his conversation with Avi.

He looked down at his purple notebook cover. He watched the blackboard and the words Miss Eisenreich now wrote:

Peter Stuyvesant...New Amsterdam...Dutch Fur Trading Conglomerate. All the meaning in his life was gone.

"Jeremiah, what's *wrong*?" Miss Eisenreich said when she turned to face the class. "What happened?" she said, and he started sobbing. He drank big, anguished gulps of air. "What happened?" she asked the class this time. "You can go to the bathroom if you need..." Miss Eisenreich stood with her arms and wrists bent in, jammed up with the rest of her body like a witness to an accident.

Jeremiah stumbled out the classroom door. He stumbled down the stairs and across the hall to the boys' room. Slamming down the towel dispenser crank three, four, five times, he tore a monster wad and scoured his snot-soaked face with the dry brown paper. He cursed himself in the mirror first, and then he cursed God.

"Fuck you, God! Why the fuck did you do this to me? *Again!*" And he felt better.

He pushed the handle three more times, gently, and ran the paper towel under warm water to clean his face.

Cleaner, drier, and more collected, Jeremiah gazed at the mirror. He focused all the attention he had, looking back at himself and speaking to God.

"God, I'm sorry. I'm sorry, God, but please..." And he felt the familiar soreness spread in his throat. "Bring her back. I'll do my homework. *Anything.*" He said it like a dare. "*You'll* see. This time I swear."

Epa Log

The Dark Lady Samantha was arrested that night. A legion of Hell's minions—shrouded, eyeless souls—led by the merciless Dark Lord Jeremiah, seized her in their lair and brought her before the Grand Tribunal assembled at his behest with the emperor's sanction. (His Excellency sat to the side on a throne of human skulls, his own head a big white skull with burning red coal eyes.) The charges were treason, espionage, insubordination. Not to mention behavior unbecoming of a Lady to the Dark Lord.

Jeremiah would preside as judge, jury, and more if he saw fit—but then, there was nowhere to go but back to Hell, and they didn't want her. So he found her guilty of everything and banished her forever. He sent her back home to Miss Eisenreich, Dr. Franny, and Mr. Schechter, back to social studies and math and homework, back to her parents.

There was power in his ruthlessness. Jeremiah felt it now. He knew this was a terrible fate for her. She deserved the worst.

INTERLUDE II

"You're two now," his dad said the first time Jeremiah got smacked. "Almost three." Was he? He had a few months still. "You're old enough to know not to do things like that." And he did do things he shouldn't do, which he knew were bad.

Like the time a few months later, after they visited his grandma. He was running around downstairs in the lobby of her building while his parents spoke to the woman his father had hired for her. His dad told him to stop running. He stopped, and went to make baby noises at his baby sister, Rachel, in her navy blue carriage. After a few minutes Jeremiah forgot he wasn't supposed to run. When he got to the tall lamp (it was an "antique," he would learn, which meant it was old, much older than him) with the "china vase" for a neck, four iron legs, and a bar that he could reach, it looked so big he thought he could swing from it like a jungle gym.

It crashed to the side of him. Before he could cry on his own his dad pulled him up and the cold marble floor on his cheek fell away in three hard smacks.

It wasn't that it hurt *so* bad, or not for so long. Soon he'd only feel it sitting down, and just for two or three days. Unless he thought about what happened. When he remembered he could feel it a little for weeks.

Even if it was an accident, Jeremiah knew it was his fault, and his dad had to pay for the lamp. But sometimes his dad got mad at him for no reason. A few months later they were all in the car, driving back after a day with his mom's parents at their golf club in Scarsdale. While Jeremiah swam all morning in his floaties, and sat by pool with Rachel and his mom and his grandpa and other grandma, eating grilled cheese sandwiches, blowing big and small bubbles in his chocolate milk with a big green straw—the kind he liked, that he could bend and stretch in and out to make popping sounds—while he swam and ate and blew bubbles and stretched and popped his straw, his dad was inside on the phone with his mom.

In the car on the ride back (it was his dad's old BM Duvvelyoo, a present from Grandma Ester for finishing law school), Jeremiah's mom asked his dad what they talked about. His grandma didn't like the woman. She said the woman was stealing her things. His dad didn't know if it was true but said he'd look for someone else. For the rest of the ride they were quiet.

They pulled into the driveway of their new building. His mom opened her door and climbed out. His dad leaned forward to kill the engine. His mom reached in from outside the back door and jerked the lever to move his dad and pull Rachel up out of her car seat.

The seat shot forward and his dad's hand caught. He yelled, turned around.

"WHAT…IS…THE…MATTER WITH YOU! WHAT…IS… THE…MATTER WITH YOU!" His father shook him against the back seat. His face was not his face.

"Allen, stop!" said his mom. "It was *me*."

His dad let go of him. He turned to Jeremiah's mom and—in a softer voice—repeated the question. Then she yelled at him, and he yelled back, and Rachel cried as Jeremiah opened his door (carefully), and noticing then that his pants were wet, he escaped to the lobby.

Years later, recalling what he could, Jeremiah remembered certain things vividly. He remembered the incident in the car; the words his dad shouted. He remembered how, when his father shook him, he had slammed against the seat in rhythm with his shouting. He remembered his mother rescuing him, and realizing that he'd pissed himself.

When he wrote about what he remembered, or what he believed he remembered, Jeremiah still had to account for certain things that he could not. So he wrote about spending the morning at the club with his mom's parents (he had many times, but whether on that day he could only guess). He added the phone call, which wasn't a shot in the dark so much as a partial surrender. He never abandoned truth, but took shortcuts—wormholes collapsing impossible distances between memories scattered like stars.

"I love you, Jair," his father said.

Jeremiah was home with his parents. He sat on the rug in the living room playing with his wooden blocks. His parents watched from the couch while his sister slept in his mother's arms.

"Jair Bear?"

"I don't love you."

It was quiet. Jeremiah kept building his tower.

"Yes, you do. Don't say that."

"No, I don't. I love Mommy."

His mom was quiet. He wanted to look at her, but never looked up from the blocks.

"I love you anyway," his dad said.

"I don't want you to love me."

"I still do."

PART II

Does the body rule the mind or does the mind rule the body?
I don't know.

Morrissey

CHAPTER FIVE
Unity

He withheld the information several days, spent hours rehearsing his speech, and stumbled over his words in a sorry attempt to spin his talk with the Dean of First Year Students several days before in the faint light of some false hope. He hadn't *failed* three classes; he'd received three "incompletes." Jeremiah would have a chance to appeal, he assured them, as though he believed his chances were good.

Notwithstanding his failure to convince them, or himself, they all stayed calm, his father remarkably so. If he worked at all to restrain himself, Jeremiah detected no effort.

Jeremiah's latest achievement had been something special. His GPA was the lowest of all in his class of five hundred. His mother nodded along, but when she sought to congratulate him ("That's great, Jeremiah," she said), his father said, "Laura, please. Okay?" Then he turned back to Jeremiah—shocked yes, devastated perhaps, but calm—and listened again.

His father's composure surprised Jeremiah at first. Afterward, when he thought it through, it made sense.

His father had changed since that night on the beach. He had less to say about things. He was deflated, his moral authority cut down, and Jeremiah took notice. He was different now, too. Everything with his father had changed somehow, he knew, and with that change a revolution started. A tyranny had been vanquished; lines were redrawn.

In the power vacuum that ensued, the insurgency that

replaced the old regime would soon collapse. His grades crapped out in the spring before college. He started smoking weed daily. He smoked before, after, or during school, and even got fired from his summer job at the New Hampshire boys' camp of his youth. The director of Merrimoose in Wortworth, New Hampshire, let him go the second week of camp on allegations of "negligence" and "inappropriate conduct" (he'd been reprimanded several times for tardiness, smoking cigarettes in the woods, and "acting stoned in the counselor shack").

Finally, after one shameful, pathetic semester at college, they sent him back home. They sent him back for a year to "gather his thoughts," in the words of the dean, who believe it or not had a rocky start in college, too, owing to a "rebellious streak" (hell, he grew up in the sixties). He too had borne the weight of successful parents. His father ran the clandestine torture wing of the CIA—something like that. Jeremiah's "demons" were similar to the deans. He sure could empathize, that dean. The dean was an empathy machine.

Jeremiah needed "a break." To "find himself." That's what the dean "recommended" He "recommended" Jeremiah "resign his enrollment" for one full year. The dean submitted his "recommendation" to the committee of faculty weighing Jeremiah's fate. All present agreed—everyone but Jeremiah's dad. Not to mention Jeremiah.

Her given name was Priscilla; she preferred Pixie.

Pixie was a junior, two classes ahead of Jeremiah and three years his senior. She was tallish, five seven or eight, and slender— muscular, sleek like a cat. Her brisk, deliberate movements and her bright green eyes were feline, too. She was from Nashville. The lisping lilt of her accent tickled him.

Her outfits stuck out in the crowds of sweatpants, spandex, and high-riding jeans. The miniskirts and leather pants she wore, her cerulean and violet eyeshadow and dark lipstick raised eyebrows all over campus. For Jeremiah—a scruffy, buzz-cut New Yorker with ripped jeans and a wallet chain, now stuck in a three-dimensional J-Crew-catalogue hell—Pixie's brand of vulgar was appealing.

In the course of weeks she'd stop by his room, or he'd visit hers. They'd listen to dark, angry music. At night she'd hang out in the downstairs common room with her friend the RA, and Jeremiah's closest pal, Guillermo Kobayashizusan—half-Japanese from Rio.

They'd kill the lights and switch on a strobe and Jeremiah would watch the three of them break out in fits of pulsing trance. Guillermo would hop like a dancing toad, whipping his ponytail and flapping red bell-bottoms. Pixie would grind against the air; she'd pump her fists; she'd drop, bounce up again, and Jeremiah would lock eyes with her in flashing stills.

Soon she confided in him about her battles with leukemia. It started in middle school. She was treated at St. Jude's, and recovered for years until it spread again, more aggressively, her last year in high school. She had to leave college for the second semester of her freshman year, which explained—though she was twenty-one—why she was still a junior. She lost her hair from the chemo and radiation. Her face bloated up. She was sure she would die the second time, but after another sickening trial of treatments, she recovered.

After she told him—before they'd ever kissed—he imagined their marriage and her funeral. It all blended in the same montage: the wedding in Kentucky at her family home on the prairie fading to Jeremiah sobbing by her bed, anointing her hospital shrouds (the machines that could not save her moaned in piercing monotone), then the immaculate corpse of her laid bare in the old white Southern Baptist Church with the black gospel choir.

She *was* Southern Baptist, or at least he thought she was.

He imagined raising their children alone when she died. He pictured the sorrow, the sympathy.

He knew just why she was there the night she opened the door to his room,

Her fragrance followed her in. He eyed the skirted curve of her sprinter's ass, her tight round hips and long white legs in brown leather boots. She hung up her lavender coat by the door and sat with him on the edge of the bed. "The Downward Spiral" blared from his speakers. They looked off at the wall, away from each other. They were silent for two full songs.

Finally, he caressed her leg, and she turned and looked straight at him. Her face moved up against his face. Their foreheads pressed, but she did not kiss him yet.

Instead she sprung up onto him and wrapped her boots around his back. Legs tangled with arms, arms with legs; noses rubbed noses, chins kissed foreheads, fingers met tongues and teeth and thumbs explored ear caverns. Temples and torsos twisted in friction faster and faster like by combining forces they could break the skin barrier, touch souls.

Soon they would kiss. Soon his hand would traverse the electric silk of her thighs up her skirt. He would peel and shuck her layers off until she was stark bare and her thighs would part for him like seas.

"Oh, Jesus Christ," she said, and then she sang out Jeremiah's name against the thrashing beat while Trent was shouting, "GOD IS DEAD."

"Do you believe in God?" he asked one night as they lay in her bed.

"I believe in something," she said.

"What's something like?"

She told a story about a race she ran her senior year in high school. She'd been sick the whole year, and was forced to miss a lot of events. To make matters worse, her doctors had recently determined that the cancer was spreading in her again. She would go in for tests the next week; this was her last chance to redeem a year in which many predicted she'd shine, even dominate several events. She began the year ranked second statewide among all sprinters. Now, at the state finals, Pixie barely qualified to run the 400 alone with a wild-card berth.

"I was real nervous before it started. I was scared I had leukemia again—which I did—and I hadn't competed all year basically. And I remember this one girl in the race who everyone thought would beat me even before I got sick that year, and she'd slaughtered everyone in pretty much every race she ran the whole season. This girl had these massive legs. She was a gazelle. All hairy too, I'll bet. Like you."

She bit a tuft of ginger bristles on his chest. They laughed. He pulled her closer, kissed her firm and gentle on the cheek. He lingered there; released. Her head settled back on his chest.

"I knew I was basically fucked, but I wanted to win so much, just this one race. I could see all the pain behind and ahead of me and I *needed* this. So I said 'please,' like to whoever would listen. 'Please, just this race.'

"Then when everyone lined up to take our marks, everything just went still. It got real quiet all the sudden, and I heard this voice. It was a feminine voice, but deep and resonant, and the voice said, 'Priscilla, relax. You will win this race.' And after that I got real calm, and the race and everyone around me kinda came back, you know, like the world just stopped for a second and started up again—like a movie almost. Then I heard the shot, and I tore out that gate like never before. I took the lead and doubled it and that was that."

"You won?"

"I beat her ass. State champion." She cupped her breast in mock humility.

A few seconds passed. "That is something."

Jeremiah could think of at least two problems, though he preferred not to, and avoided the temptation whenever he could.

Still, he could not shake the thought that all this recreation and intrigue left little time for work. When he thought of the classes he'd missed, and of the enormous debt of work he owed, the thought was so absurd and overwhelming he would cut it off at the string like a giant fire balloon in a windstorm. He hoped it would burst somewhere else.

The second problem was his girlfriend back home. Jeremiah had met Sasha in high school the year before and there, in high school, Sasha remained in her senior year.

Sasha was Jeremiah's first love—he really had loved her, and he still did.

It was the drugs mostly. After his first mushroom trip Jeremiah told her about the experience, how incredible it was. He'd discovered so much about himself, about life. He wished he could remember it. Sasha waited until he was done to start crying.

He no longer looked forward to her calls. She'd become another task for him, like the homework he was neglecting. With Pixie there was no work, no explaining. She was much better suited for the new Jeremiah than his old girlfriend was, he believed, but something kept him from ending things as he knew he should. He understood it had something to do with Pixie.

As fraught as the whole thing was for him, Pixie didn't consider his lingering girlfriend problem to be a problem at all. On the contrary, she seemed to like the idea of Sasha. Pixie would often ask about her with friendly interest. Her apparent lack of jealousy both impressed and bothered him.

One night before a psych test, when Jeremiah was forced to deal with the massive pile of work now poised to collapse and bury him, he went to the library. It was a final, desperate resort (he'd been in the library twice, once for his orientation tour). He tried to study there for an hour or so, but much like Socrates, the more he read, the less he understood, and the panic rose in Jeremiah's chest. He packed up his books, marched to the exit, and jogged over to Pixie's room.

He lay down on her bed, dropped his head in her lap. He huffed and moaned, hiding his eyes from the light she read by. He fought the urge to cry, successfully, and instead he said, "You've been so good to me. You make me happier. I don't see any point to the time I spend without you." He wanted to say the rest, but resisted without knowing why.

The damage was done, though. Jeremiah sensed he had violated some unspoken code. He felt it in her body's stillness; he heard in her silence.

They'd spent the night apart; although they'd had no agreement to meet, he had expected her. She'd spent the night with his pal, Guillermo, her comrade in techno dance.

Unbeknownst to Jeremiah, Guillermo, Pixie, and her friend the RA had congregated in the common room downstairs to dance. Then Guillermo and Pixie danced back to his room and screwed—as he later learned—on the top bunk while, below, Guillermo's roommate faked sleep.

Pixie was ashamed. She was truly, desperately sorry. She knew she'd hurt him. She hoped he'd somehow find it in his heart…She started crying.

He thought about killing his friend. He imagined beating Guillermo's head to a red wet stump beneath his boot heel. Jeremiah knew he had no right to feel this way, that he was a hypocrite. He knew he should have expected it. He did not deserve the love of one woman, let alone two. He knew if a cosmic order were found it should spurn the likes of him—in all fairness—and there he found a certain comfort.

"What up, bro? I'm Tino."

Tino guided Jeremiah through an elaborate ritual of thumbs, sliding palms, and a finger-snap on the release. He was darkish, thin with jet-black hair. A silver hoop impaled his lower lip.

"How you doin', sweetheart?" Tino kissed Rachel on the cheek. One of her crazy friends had dated him, prior to the girl's stint in a psychiatric ward after a clumsy suicide attempt (she'd swallowed too many painkillers, but only enough to make her throw up a lot). Tino was sixteen, and lived with his folks in a cluttered prewar tenement flat just a few blocks from them. Jeremiah was there to buy acid.

The room smelled like cat piss. It was dirty and small; one window faced a brick wall over an alley. "Princess," a fat brown cat, sized them up with yellow carnivorous eyes from her windowsill perch. The apartment surprised Jeremiah. He hadn't known one like this could still exist in his neighborhood.

"How's Ananda?" Tino looked at Rachel all serious.

She frowned back. "Okay. I guess."

"Glad to hear. I still feel kinda bad, you know. She's a real sweet girl, n' shit. I still wanna be friends with her, you know, but right now it's like…you know how it is."

"How is it?"

Tino flinched a little bit. He seemed unaccustomed to follow-ups. "I don't know. She's kinda fucked up. You know?"

Rachel looked down, satisfied. "Yeah," she said.

"I know she's your friend and all, though." His thought seemed to end there.

Tino's pager went off. He had to take the call. He dialed.

"Yo, what up, bro? Word? Ah, shit, for real? *Shit*, bro, that's fucked up. What can I say? I'm mad sorry."

Jeremiah looked at his sister. They smirked. Tino's half of the conversation continued.

"Uh huh…word, I hear you, bro…uh huh…no doubt. Aight, bro, check it out. Juss come by in like thurdy, uh su'in, I'll hook you up mad nice…yeah, bro, don't worry…*word*. It's the goods. It's all good, homes. I see you then. *Peace*."

He hung up.

"Sorry, guys. This dude got robbed at this club last night and they took his glass. It's not my problem, really, but I sold him the shit and he's a good customer, so I'll probably toss him a deal, throw in a bag for free or some shit. He's kinda wack, though. I'm not surprised he got robbed. Little prep school bitch." Tino laughed.

"Hey!" Rachel slapped him on the arm. Tino laughed harder.

"What's glass?" Jeremiah said. "Like a pipe? For weed?"

"Nah, bro—methamphetamine. Glass is like a concentrated form of crystal. One little bump you'll be tweakin' fa ouwiz. I danced *six* ouwiz *straight* at this rave down in Philly last weekend, bro. Off the *hook*. I ain't lyin.'"

Jeremiah had never tried crystal.

"It must be exhausting for you to talk that way."

"What way?"

"You know, like that. For a whole conversation. You must get tired."

Tino looked confused.

"Never mind." Jeremiah grinned and looked away. Rachel laughed. "So how much for the tabs?"

"How many you guys need?" Now Tino looked suspicious.

Jeremiah had never tried acid. He looked at his sister. She shrugged. He turned to Tino. "How strong are these?"

"These are Black *Widows*, bro." He took out a Ziploc bag with a small sheet covered in cartoon spiders.

"Will one and a half be enough?"

"Wit' dese, no doubt." Tino's eyes bugged out to demonstrate.

He ripped five tabs from the sheet and stuffed them in a tiny blue plastic baggie. Jeremiah exchanged twenty-five dollars for it. Tino invited them to go with him to Unity at Vinyl (a.k.a. The Shelter) the following Friday. It was the same club where the guy got robbed the night before. They shouldn't worry though, he said, because normally it was mad safe, and besides, Tino knew one of the bouncers.

His sister had other plans that night; Jeremiah might like to go.

The Shelter was dark and deafening, an assault of rapid-fire beats and mortars of electric noise. Sirens erupted; screams from the floor harmonized with the bass pounding four beats unrelenting—so loud the vibrations struck his chest and the bass merged with his pulse, stronger with each strobe-lit snapshot of writhing, rapturous bodies—and lasers probed the fog that poured from hidden valves. This was Unity.

Tino started to dance. His feet rode the crest of drums while his fingers trailed violet strands, leading first with the right, then the left, his body sinuous with snaking hands. Tino was good at this. Soon others were watching, and Tino fed off the attention. His moves got faster and more intricate. One hand stopped while the other went behind his head, circled around his neck and jerked up in a fist along with his chin, like he'd hanged himself. The movement provoked surprise, laughter from bystanders. He cracked invisible whips and cocked invisible hammers to shotguns conjured from the air.

Later, Tino handed him a cigarette. The thing was damp, though, and it smelled like nail polish.

"WHAT THE FUCK IS THIS?" He yelled so Tino could hear.

"IT'S A DIP."

"A WHAT?"

"DUST, BRO. PCP."

"ARE YOU SERIOUS?!"

"RELAX. JUST TAKE ONE PUFF."

Tino took the drenched Newport, sparked it, exhaled the smoke, then passed it back to him. Jeremiah wouldn't know how to describe what he felt next, except to say that he no longer felt human, or mammal even, but more like a reptile. He sat like a log in a swamp, floating, while Tino—who had bagged up some K at Jeremiah's place—cruised The Shelter for customers. Jeremiah watched the bouncing waifs in sports bras and wide-legged jeans, little girls with blue and bright red hair, with bare midriffs and silvery navels. These rainbow sprites were from another world. They were not for reptiles.

Tino wanted to bring back a few "heads" to Jeremiah's "crib" to "cook up some licks and chill." He had no idea what a lick might be, or how one was cooked; he barely knew Tino, let alone whoever Tino wanted to bring to his parents' "crib." Still, exhausted as he was, he did not want to sleep.

"Sup, bro?" Tino said. "Thanks for letting us chill."

"Word," said Mecca. "Your folks got a phat crib, cuz."

Jeremiah luxuriated outside on the terrace with three of his new friends. Mecca was tall, possessed of the gaunt and sickly physique of an alien sorcerer in space jeans, and a black, caftan-like Adidas shirt with shoulder stripes. His ethnic makeup was indeterminate, some mix gone jaundice yellow-green.

Richie, the other one—powder pale—looked down at his knees and said nothing. He did not acknowledge his host. There was little evidence to suggest Richie was aware of anything outside himself, or that he was alive. Then Tino and Mecca started talking about "gear."

"It's fuckin' wack, the shit people wear these days, these fuckin' polo rave-uhs," interjected Richie from beyond the grave.

"Back in the day, you know, like five yeaz ago at the Shadow Raves? Back den you neva sawr a single fuckin' polo shirt."

The resurrection was complete. Richie was back to set things right for the not-yet-dead.

"Rave-uhs were real back den, not a bunch of faggy label hoaz." Richie and Mecca were both gay.

"Yo, chill, bro." Tino caressed the hem of his polo shirt in apology for his asshole friend who had gone too far. "This shirt is phat."

"No, Tino, I'm sorry. I love you, bro—"

"Chill, B."

"I *love* you, Tino, but it's fuckin' wack. I'm sorry. Yous only been goin' ta parties fa like two yeaz, so you dunno. If you were dere dough, like back in the *day*. *Den* you'd *know*."

"Whatevers."

"Why does it matter what people wear at all?" said Jeremiah.

Richie eyed Jeremiah's pseudo-skater-punk rags with

disdain. He hadn't seemed to notice till then that Jeremiah wore clothes.

"Because when you put on gear, you're saying, 'I'm a rave-uh, yo. *Dis* is who I am.' And when you walk around like some po-za fuckin' label ho-a, yous misrepresentin'. This shit ain't some fad."

Jeremiah thought someone should let Richie know how stupid he sounded, for his own good. But for reasons at which he could guess only, he preferred to impress these philosophers. So he said nothing.

One weekend, after some prodding, Jeremiah agreed to join his sisters and parents up at the country house. On Saturday afternoon his mother asked to talk to him—but not just a regular talk, like about theater tickets, dinner dates with his grandparents, health forms, or dental appointments. This time she wanted him in the basement. Which was odd, since normally it was his father who detained him behind closed doors to "talk."

She flipped the switch. He followed her down the wooden steps, past the washer and dryer. His mother wore her weekend getup: tennis sneakers, grey sweatpants, and a purple and puce tie-dyed *Johnston Class of '68* reunion shirt—his dad's, so it draped down over her thighs.

Maybe she'd lose her shit and attack him. It had happened once with her, three or four years before, also at the house. She was telling him to stop bothering Rachel, or Lisa, or both, which one or both of them kept whining about, and the next thing he knew his mom was kicking him and hammer-fisting his chest. Jeremiah stumbled backward to his room. When they reached it, he squared up to her and showed her the back of his hand.

His mother flinched. "I'm gonna tell your father."

She did, but his dad just took him aside and told him about the time he was around Jeremiah's age, fourteen or fifteen, and his mother tried to slap him but he raised his arm to block and she hurt her hand. His father took him aside and said *never raise a hand to your mother*, and when Jeremiah's dad said he hadn't, that he only raised his hand to block—it was an instinct, what was he supposed to do?—his dad's dad said, "Next time, let her."

He delivered the tale with a knowing smile. The subtext seemed to be that women would be women, and sometimes they would attack you for no special reason—irrational creatures—and not to worry. In other words, Jeremiah might as well forget it happened. Because she would. And wasn't Jeremiah the luckiest boy to have such a cool dad?

He was ready for her now as she led him through the basement. He could take anything she threw at him. If she yelled, he could yell louder.

When she turned around, his mom was crying.

"It's been very hard for me to see you looking so unhappy," she said. "And I know we've grown apart. But I just wanted you to know that Daddy and I are here for you. If you're ever in trouble, or anything else you need from us. And if we're hard on you sometimes it's because we care, and we love you very much."

He knew they did. On some level that made it worse.

CHAPTER SIX
Coke Is It!

The thing about crystal meth was how it made everything possible for a few minutes.

It was that and how the more you used, the less you needed to sleep—the less you slept, the more you knew you were never alone.

The first night maybe you saw one here, one there, somewhere off in the corner. After two or three nights they filled the room and followed you out. On four, five nights without sleep, they surrounded you. The shadow people sat on stoops. They crouched behind cars and leaned against streetlamps. They ran past you, ahead of you, and across your path. You saw or heard them in whispers, or else you just knew they were there. Were they the ones who made him do the things he did?

That was why Jeremiah liked company when he got high. Real people, flesh and blood bodies kept the ghosts away. People like Mary.

He met her one Friday night at his parents' apartment. She had danced in the second company of the Joffrey Ballet. She attended a state college in Westchester, thirty minutes' drive from the city. She was tall and gaunt and pale and beautiful, with short, dark hair. She had big round eyes, emerald and amber moons that called to him—without even looking at him—from the couch across the room.

A regular crew began to materialize around him. It material-ized around Tino, in truth, though usually in Jeremiah's superior and parentless apartment. They were all there on the weekends before, after, or instead of the clubs. They blasted techno, popped pills, and blew lines of whatever Tino was carrying. The mainstays were Tino and Lea, his girl, Pedro and B.J.—who he'd met on the scene through Tino—and now, at last, there was Mary.

Pedro from the Bronx was seventeen. He was shortish, five seven at most. He was fit, muscular Jeremiah guessed, but then so was Jane Fonda. Pedro fixed his hair in the mirror a lot, and danced a lot, and sometimes danced while fixing his hair in the mirror. Pedro wrote poetry, too (his first novel, which he would write with "mad poetry," would be called *Drawn from the Fingers of Fire*). Whenever Pedro tweaked on glass he annexed the bathroom for hours. Whoever went in after would find an entire roll stuffed in the small basket and none left to use. His navel was pierced and prone to infection, he said.

Then there was B.J., a homeless raver from Albany with a blond soul patch to match his bleached Mohawk. The barbell in his eyebrow loomed largest of a half-dozen piercings in his face; twin baby-bells through the rim of each ear looked like the silver lodged in the flesh above his eye had spawned quadruplets. He was almost always broke, relying on girlfriends to put him up at their parents' places. He danced a lot, too—B.J. and Pedro were both adepts at the liquid rave style, though not on Tino's level. B.J. preferred K to glass, even though every time he sunk into the hole he borrowed or stole for he looked paralyzed and suicidal (he drooled a lot, and his glazed and absent eyes leaked tears).

B.J. never stole from Jeremiah, or Jeremiah believed he did not, or he never questioned him at least—not even when two laptops, two silver watches, and two fur coats went missing from his parents' home after one party. But there had been over fifty people there that night, many he did not know at all, and some who seemed much sketchier than B.J.

Incredibly, Jeremiah's parents kept going away, and leaving him home, and letting him throw parties. That he did not understand.

B.J. did borrow a lot from Jeremiah, and only sometimes paid him back. And even while Jeremiah understood that B.J., free spirited as he was, did not shame easily, and while Jeremiah had observed that B.J. operated as though he were wholly unburdened with conventional feelings of guilt and responsibility, he seldom complained.

Mary had his trust, a rare commodity in the world he had entered. He understood that now. A month before he was in love with Samsara, Lea's old roommate—a diminutive redhead bursting with neurotic energy. She was cooing and flirty with him. She'd ask Jeremiah to pick up grocery items for her on the way, and he never asked for money. Soon she stopped offering, and showered him with praise instead. She touched him a lot, and nestled up on his arm like a happy, hungry little pug.

One day Samsara mused to Lea about how nice it was to have Jeremiah around. It was great, she said, since now their refrigerator was always stocked. When Lea told him what Samsara said, Jeremiah did not react.

Tino and Lea looked at each other. They looked back at him.

"Don't you think that's fucked up, bro?" said Tino.

Lea raised her brows. The rim of her blue raving visor nodded up and down.

"Why?" said Jeremiah. "I like doing favors for friends. It feels good to me."

"No doubt, 'cause you're mad sweet, n' all. But she's using you, bro."

Lea nodded again—bigger, slower nods.

The revelation stung. It was hard for him to understand. Not the obvious fact that people could actually be like this but that someone might use *him*, Jeremiah, this way. His friends at college never did. Most of his high school friends were as spoiled as he was. Sometimes more.

The thought hardly crossed his mind, which was why Jeremiah "loaned" B.J. money, knowing well he'd never see most of it back. He was lucky to have the money he had, he reasoned—money he'd earned working, and more from his parents—and it made Jeremiah feel needed and loved to spread the wealth. Besides, he bought drugs for Mary now. Jeremiah did not want her to believe his generosity was selective.

Mary did not like Samsara. Samsara was sketchy, Mary said; she did not deserve Jeremiah's friendship. She said all this very early one morning while they crushed up the dregs of the crystals in the bag he'd bought for them that night. If Mary couldn't afford to get high, Jeremiah took care of her. She hesitated always. And no little touches and shoulder nestlings— no grand declarations. Mary just thanked him gently with a kind of solemn gratitude. They both knew she would never repay him.

They joked a lot about B.J. Mary hooked up with him one night early in the summer. B.J. went back to his ex-girlfriend the next day, crying and begging forgiveness for nothing in particular. Yvette, a tiny, gorgeous brunette, was fifteen, and her parents despised B.J. She could not resist him, though, and snuck him upstairs, and within a few days B.J. had spent all the money he'd saved "working" (he'd cooked up a lick of K and sold a dozen bags at a club for Tino the week before) to have "Yvette" tattooed in red cursive across his lower back. The next night, for reasons apparently unrelated, Yvette dumped him again. Once B.J. was finished crying and shouting, Mary looked at him and laughed.

Jeremiah's conversations with Mary almost always turned to drugs. They did with all his new friends. They discussed the drugs they were taking; the drugs they liked most; the various memorable times they'd been fucked up on this or that drug and how it was getting harder all the time to get good shit from good people. The scene was getting too sketchy. That was the consensus. And it wasn't even about the music anymore—just money and drugs.

Jeremiah walked along Central Park late one night with Lea, Tino, and Mary. Lea would stay at Tino's that night, and Mary, not wanting to go back to Westchester, needed a place to stay, too. She had planned on staying at Tino's.

"Why don't you stay with Jeremiah?" Lea asked. She smiled at Jeremiah. Mary said nothing.

They crossed the street at Tino's block. Tino and Lea crossed first and Mary dropped back with him. She looked upset.

"What's wrong?" he said.

"Lea. She's acting like they wanna get rid of me. I understand if they want some privacy. All she had to do was ask."

"Well," he smiled at her, "I think maybe that was more for my benefit than hers."

She looked away.

When they got to Tino's building, Lea asked Mary where she wanted to stay. Mary said she'd stay at Tino's, if that was okay with them.

When he stopped by the next day Mary was curled up on Tino's bed. She looked miserable. She watched him silently. He wondered if she could talk, if she tried. He looked over at Tino and Lea.

"What happened?" Jeremiah asked. He heard the anger in his voice.

"We did some K last night," said Tino.

"Had she ever done it?"

"Once, I think," said Lea. "She was a mess last night but she's better now. She hasn't slept, though."

Jeremiah looked at Tino. "Are you okay?" he asked Mary. He turned and she nodded vaguely. He wanted to lie with her on the bed. He wanted to wrap her in his arms, squeeze the poison out. She closed her eyes and shrunk back deep within herself.

"She's a-ight, bro," said Tino.

Jeremiah said goodbye. He'd stop in again later.

When he left Tino's building the light of the cloudless summer afternoon warmed his skin. He started to cry. He had not shed a tear in several years.

They built slowly at first, falling one at a time. At home they flowed freely, though still quietly. He did not sob. He was devastated; he wanted her so much that not having her hurt him physically (his throat was sore and something clenched up in his chest). Still he was calm, or enough to sit down at his desk and compose his "Song for a Sad, Fallen Angel."

He copied the poem to a clean sheet of paper from his notebook. He wrote slowly, with excruciating care for every character of his transcription. Twice he cursed aloud, ripped up the page and started fresh. On the third attempt he was satisfied. He folded the poem up in a beige envelope with his name and address, the customized stationery a relic of his college application days—and, he believed, the perfect touch. He wrote her name on the front, passed out in bed, and woke in a panic. He looked at his clock: five hours had passed. He hoped she hadn't gone away.

Mary was still at Tinos when he arrived again. She looked much better now. She was up and ready to head back to school. He walked her out and to the corner. Here they would separate. He gave her the envelope.

"Just something I wrote for you."

She smiled at him, and kissed him on the forehead, which gave him hope since normally she just kind of stuck out her cheek at him.

He hadn't heard from her that week. He didn't dare call, or even discuss what he'd done, not even with Lea.

That Thursday Lea told him she and Tino were taking the train up to visit Mary. Lea said Mary told her she'd like to see Jeremiah, too.

The next twenty-four hours were tortured bliss. The thought of what he'd done nearly made him nauseous. He'd revealed everything, *everything*, he thought. It seemed there was nothing about him she couldn't know from what he'd written. There was no mystery left to him.

But so what, he thought. People should say what they felt. They should speak from the heart, but instead people talked about shit that meant nothing to hide their feelings. Not Jeremiah—no sir.

And what had he risked, really? His pride?

It could be *really* embarrassing.

What if she pitied him?

What if she mocked him?

He would strangle her.

God, what was wrong with him?

What would he *do*?

How could he ever face her again?

How could he possibly?

With courage, was how. If Mary didn't love him she would at least respect him—and maybe, just maybe, his poetic genius, or the sheer blind force of his devotion to her, would tip the balance.

When they moved in together he would stay home and write, or smoke a joint while she danced in the studio he would build for her to start dancing again. She'd stand behind him while he wrote, massaging him, *luring* him to bed as he raced to finish a powerful sentence.

Jeremiah stood off to the side of her door. When it opened, he did not want her to see him right away. He felt it would be better to prolong the mystery. He couldn't say why.

She kissed Tino and Lea first before she looked his way. He wasn't sure what to make of the look she gave him then, but despised it. Her eyes told him everything in that moment. It was more question than answer. What did he expect, maybe, and would he really make her explain it to him?

"Hi," she said, and stuck out her cheek.

That night they took ecstasy. A DJ friend of Mary's she'd fucked a few times spun house records in his room. The guy was kind of fat, kind of sloppy. He didn't look like much to Jeremiah, though he was a DJ.

They were rolling hard and sprawled on the floor when Mary found him. He awoke to himself sitting with her—in front of her, between and against her legs. She rubbed his shoulders. His thumbs massaged her calves beneath her jeans. He touched her with singular focus, channeling from deep and vast reserves, and through his fingertips he surrendered everything to her.

Mary's touch was warm. It was soothing and kind. Jeremiah searched her hands for desire. He searched, and would keep searching for weeks, then months and years, revisiting that night. He'd return for clues and answers first, then for memory's sake alone, fixing the moment's crystalline form.

The records played for hours and hours, then stopped. The sun rose.

Hours later Jeremiah left Grand Central Station alone. He followed his feet west. When he reached Times Square, he looked up. And here's what he saw: tank-sized luxury sedans, ballistic rockets of Heineken bottles, and anorexic giants in lingerie staring down through long black lashes. Clocks on a building façade broadcast the time in a dozen world capitals he cared nothing about. Stock listings that meant nothing to him streaked by on a digital banner. A yellow fog rose from the giant coffee mug and thinned out over the square—over the raging yellow river of cabs, the warring tribes of tourists, and the raised platform where the Black Israelites donned shiny crowns, purple robes, and tinfoil breastplates. They shouted prophesies of doom to a nation of faggots and fake white Jews. A few people watched, puzzled, but no one heard them.

The cameras were all pointed at the world's most famous electronic billboard.

COKE

Is It!

COKE

Is It!

COKE

Is It!

   Is It!

   Is It!

Is It!

Is It!

Is It!

CHAPTER SEVEN
Windows on the Void

The Towers stuck up dark and grey and merlot-stained—portals in the lavender blue that stretched forever past Lower Manhattan. The gates opened to somewhere impossibly far, past forever, like vast empty spaces where space unfolded and folded again, collapsing impossible distances.

The sun crossed the Hudson into Jersey well ahead of them. Swamp-like, they would all sink slowly there into dusk.

Sunset colored the scattered clouds, merlot and grey matching the monolithic stems at the island's stern; it sailed like a vessel through time. The Towers grew slowly. What if he could drive through the gates? The car floated up to answer his wish. That made it easier to steer. Alone. Above the traffic. And as they approached the cosmic portals Jeremiah wondered where they would take them instead of New Jersey. Somewhere back in time where he could fix whatever went wrong? To the future to see how cool everything turned out? Somewhere better? Far away? Heavenly? Too perfect to imagine? Soon they stretched over the windshield frame. The closer they got along the wide river, the more they looked like the indestructible legs of an interplanetary god.

Jeremiah hovered his parents' second car, the family minivan, with Tino up front and Pedro in back. The volume of Tino's DJ Odi jungle mix made conversation unnecessary. The party was going down tonight. He adjusted course; they would not cross the gates now. They would cross the tunnel, for the drugs, and drive back.

Which might have been a long way to drive, but tonight they needed lots of drugs, and different kinds, and the guy they knew who had lots of different drugs was in Jersey.

So what could they do?

Jeremiah had stopped the hard drugs months before. A two-week trip to Hawaii with his parents did the trick. These days he smoked a lot of weed, and that was pretty much it. But this was no ordinary party. It was mid-November; nearly a full year had passed since Jeremiah was sent home from school, and his time to return had arrived almost, at last. The dean called weeks before to tell him personally that Johnston would have him back; if he chose to return, Jeremiah would be readmitted on academic probation.

Which meant he couldn't fuck up anymore—or else.

It was time to get serious, he knew, though never without a big sendoff.

Pedro conducted beat experiments on the back of Jeremiah's seat. The song did not need more drums.

Traffic flowed effortlessly toward the feet of the great glass legs; they were back on the freeway. But Jeremiah wasn't driving now. A magnetic force pulled him. Like a Death Star tractor beam but kinder. Gentler.

Something needed saying then, he knew; it was Tino who lowered the volume.

"Wouldn't it be phat," he said, "if the world ended right now?"

When Tino said ended, it sounded like "inded." Jeremiah knew just what he meant, though.

"Word."

"Our generation will see the next stage in evolution," Samsara was saying. Jeremiah sat on the big leather easy chair in his parents' living room. Two leather couches flanked his leather throne; she sat in the one to his right with blue-hair Nicky, purple-hair Jenny, and green-hair Annie: "the Trolls." All kinds of drugs were kicking in. Jeremiah was feeling superior.

"Really?" he interjected. Samsara had been talking to the Trolls, but Jeremiah couldn't help overhearing. "How does that work?"

She looked at him.

"What's going to happen to our generation?"

"Our generation," she said again "will witness the evolution of our species."

He looked at the Trolls. They said nothing. They were ready to let this go, he guessed.

"Where did you get this idea?" he asked. "How is that possible? Evolution takes thousands of years. Millions."

"We're always evolving."

"How? What do you mean? Our bodies? Our brains?" He was mystified.

"Yeah, but also our language. And society. Like the words we use and how they are different from our parents' words. Or their generation. You know. Like the way we talk about 'vibes,' and things. We see more than them. We feel more."

She. This. Whatever *this* was. It was making sense.

"You know," she went on. "All this stuff about the millennium?"

No. He did not know.

"It's happening already. We'll see more after the millennium."

Two Trolls were nodding now. Nicky Blue Troll's eyes studied him. What did they all know that he did not?

"What if the world ends?" he heard himself say before he was aware the thought had formed. The even pulse of bass from the speaker embedded in the woodwork slowed. It sped up again.

Samsara's head cocked back and shot forward at Jeremiah again in shear perplexity.

"The world is ending right now."

Those words did something to him. When she said them something cracked wide open in his skull. He felt it. A sound like the blades of a fan or propeller spinning engulfed him from nowhere. The figures and objects surrounding him started changing, then losing their shapes entirely as the room faded. He was lifted then (there was no better word) to a place that was entirely unfamiliar to him. Not just the place; everything in it was different from anything he could remember. He could identify nothing he saw—if "seeing" was what you would call it. He recognized no *thing* at all. Kaleidoscopic swirls of shadow and light. Sound and vibration. Ghostly hints of shapes and patterns shifting at spectacular velocity so no line or color fully imprinted itself on the mind before some new impression replaced it. There was nothing solid to grasp or oppose. No lines divided the universe. None drew the universe away from him.

When the room emerged from the noise again, every-thing—the faces, the bodies, the sounds and the lights in the sky through the windowpane—had changed. He saw it now. His apartment was a spaceship in disguise. It always had been. It was waiting for him. For *them*. Where would it take them? When?

"What's the matter?" asked Nicky Blue Troll.

Her chin. Her *ears*. Her face was not her face.

"You good, hon?" Samsara now. Her face, too?

Jeremiah jumped up from the leather chair. "Just a sec."

He jogged from the living room into his bathroom, flipped the switch, and locked the door. In the mirror he first saw the face of a scared and angry troglodyte glaring at him through black eyes tucked beneath a clenched and simian brow. The next moment his features softened until he recognized the face he would call his own, or he guessed he would. Then it shifted again as the features grew longer and more defined, and longer still, narrower, sleeker, and more triangular until the face he could recognize moments before looked something more than human.

Samsara and the Trolls had moved from the couch to the dining room. They were four she-dragons, supernatural creatures mingling in a room with humans, hiding from them in plain sight.

"What the *hell* is going on?"

Samsara left the others to talk to him privately. "What is it?"

"You? Me? *This?* What's happening to me?"

"You're on acid," she said. "And a bunch of other shit. Didn't you just do a bump of K?"

"Yes," he said. "Yes, I am. I did. But *still.*"

"Still what?"

Jeremiah took a good look at her face. Was she fucking with him? Did she not see what he saw? On her own face? On his? How did his face look to her? Hers was pale, enchanted, sleek like a lizard, and yet the lines were never quite defined, not completely, but shifting constantly, imperceptibly, and casting the faintest silvery glow as though even this—this magical form—were yet another avatar and her face a silhouette framing her soul, which glowed with a faint hypnotic transparency.

"I don't know. I'm seeing all this stuff right now. I've never seen it before. And I've done acid."

"Good acid?"

"Yeah. I think so. Sure I have." He felt defensive.

"It sounds like you're realizing that you know," she said. Jenny Purple Troll was standing next to Samsara. Jenny made a beautiful, tiny purple dragon: all four feet eleven inches of her.

"What do you mean? I know what?"

"You just know."

Jenny was nodding. She flashed her fangs at him in a smile. His panic and bewilderment drew her to him like a magnet. She *liked* this?

"It's like, some people think they know," Samsara went on. "And some people just know."

"So what do I know that they think they know?"

"You just know," Jenny said. "Like, I started having all these realizations like a year ago. And that's when I knew."

Jenny would have the last word on that for now. Annie and Nicky pulled her away to go upstairs to the roof. They had a Dutch Master rolled.

Lea and Mary came over to them. He hadn't seen them all night.

"What's goin' on, Shmeremiah?" Mary said.

"You lost in your house again?" Lea asked. She attacked him with tickles, then bit his upper arm below the sleeve.

"Ouch!" he yelled.

"He's freaking out," Samsara explained. "Tripping balls."

Mary's eyes scolded him playfully. "Space cadet. Earth to Shmere-mi-ah." She kissed his forehead.

"I need to lie down," he said. "I wanna lie down. I should lie down, I think."

The four of them lay in his parents' bed, looking up at the rectangular mirror that hung on the ceiling (a longstanding source of amusement for Jeremiah and his friends). They watched themselves, watched each other watching themselves and themselves each other until he forgot who was watching what. And who? He focused again on the faces—three angelic faces transmuted, glowing, shedding sparks like they were dissolving slowly to formless, unobstructed light. And yet he could *feel* them, too. And could he ever tonight.

"What am I supposed to be doing right now?" he said to no one in particular.

Lea had this way of drawing his attention to his own absurdity without saying a word. It was in her smile—a hint of sadistic pleasure. The savagery of her affection bordered on ruthless at times. She could use her ass as a weapon and smile like a man.

"What do you mean?" Mary said. She looked suspicious.

"Like in life. What should I be doing now?"

"What do you want to do? You want to go back to college, right?"

"Yeah. I guess. I mean…" How could they think of college? Of all places. And now of all times? They must not be seeing things the way he was. "Now, though. Before then. What do I need to do? What are the things I should have?" He was planning for the imminent journey through space. He didn't know when they would launch. Or take off. Or whatever.

Samsara's eyes met his. She smiled at him. "You can have whatever you want."

I want you, he thought. I want all three of you. Now.

But he wouldn't know how to ask something like that. Not tonight. Jeremiah did ask the universe, though. And one day he would get his answer. Sure enough. And two out of three wasn't bad.

When he woke up alone in his parents' bed and noticed it was daytime, Jeremiah guessed his apartment had not been a spaceship the night before. If it was, they were still on the ground. Through the window near the bed he saw the familiar vista of pale, high-windowed fortresses at Lincoln Center surrounding the plaza and the round, black-marble fountain basin, water towers, smokestacks, fragments of the Hudson River and Jersey coast broken by West Side high-rise condos. The sky was a clear, deep blue. Against it the darker blue silhouettes of a legion of giant creatures with bat-like wings gathered in formation. Suspended, lined up in a perfect symmetry of rows and columns, they filled the expanse of sky from the horizon all the way up as high as the window went. They had no eyes that he could see. No features defined them. They were faceless blue shadows, identical, stark, united as a force and waiting. For what?

As though to answer his thought, the shadows dove laterally away from the center. Their wings spread, they glided and danced, tracing circles and arcs and twirling like synchronized swimmers competing for Armageddon. Jeremiah heard music somewhere.

The couches in the living room were filled with Trolls and other remnants of the crowd that had gathered the night before. Tino and Pablo were there. B.J. the homeless raver lay on his side, passed out in Jeremiah's favorite chair. He and Mary had been together on and off for the past several months. They were off again; he was sleeping on couches these days.

B.J. was an ass and a leach. Jeremiah saw it clear as day. He did not like to feel compelled to keep him around for Mary or his other friends, if *they* even liked him anymore. He did not want to be bitter, though. If that's what it was. Bitterness. For knowing in his heart that Mary could do so much better than *that* (if she only knew). It was the least Jeremiah could do for him, though. For her.

"What *up*, bro?" Tino got up from the couch to throw him a pound with a secret handshake. Jeremiah, for one, always improvised those. But he seemed to get the gist.

"I dunno. What's up?"

Nicky Blue Troll's fingernails were orange. He noticed that when she laughed and her hands bounced off her wide-leg raver jeans. "Look at him," she said.

"What?" Just leave me alone, he thought.

"He's so beautiful."

He stared at his face in the bathroom mirror. Was he beautiful? Blue Troll had never said so before. No one did. Several years had passed since the days when his reflection produced feelings of shame so paralyzing that he pretended sometimes he did not see himself but someone else's sad, fat, ugly face. He looked different since he lost the weight. He thought he looked pretty cool sometimes. *He* was a cool guy. Wasn't he? His reflection had no answer.

He looked different today and last night, though. More different than ever. Everyone did, to him at least, but the difference was hard to describe. It was less pronounced than it had been the night before. But the longer he watched the faces of his friends, or his own face in the mirror, while his eyes adjusted—to his madness, his new way of seeing or whatever it was that was going on right now with him, Jeremiah Levi— the more different they appeared. Part of what he was seeing involved geometry. He could see that now. He saw lines, angles, and symmetries that were always invisible to his eyes. It wasn't like their faces had really *changed*. Had they? Was that possible? Of course it was not. But Nicky noticed a change in him. Samsara noticed it, too. So something must be going on.

But it wasn't really about how he looked, maybe, or not just. He felt more vibrant—literally, like a tuning fork. Someone had flipped a switch and slowed the oscillation of spinning electrons around the atomic nuclei that cemented his being, and now he was lighter, freer, and he knew if he focused all his energy—if he gave it all up, left it behind—then nothing, not gravity itself could hold his feet to the ground.

The Sheep Meadow was closed that time of year, but he scaled the fence easily and made it to the center of the giant field in the little park on the small island on the tiny planet called Earth adrift somewhere in a galaxy of frightening dimensions, with interstellar distances too vast and empty for the mind's comforts, too big to map (the diagrams he saw in science textbooks, the models at planetariums were like the maps explorers drew in the fifteenth century), beyond the scope of our very finest cameras and telescopes fumbling around in space, groping in the dark like Prufrock's ragged claws on the floors of silent seas.

And the universe?

He could hardly imagine.

He saw it clearly, though, or he felt it looking up at the august prewar luxury towers that framed the park like jagged cliffs over the skeleton of bare tree branches. He felt the old gears of his mind shifting and the knots in his soul as they loosened one after the other, effortless, with the slightest suggestion of word or thought, and he knew that the universe shifted with him, and uncoiled with him, and he knew he was the universe, and he knew the universe would get where it was going. It was the nature of things. All he could do was keep pace with it. Or set the pace, since all of creation would never be free without him. And Jeremiah would never be free without creation. He looked upon it then, on creation, on the West Side of Babylon. He saw that it was good.

Too bad it would all end soon—this view of creation. The world as it was would end. He saw it clearly and saw his part in it. He could feel the sheetrock flesh of the black lizard that grew in him beneath the pale soft skin the world saw. It would tear through any moment now. At the appointed hour. His wings would break the cosmetic flesh; he would shed his old skin like an undershirt; he and the others, his friends, and the rest like them would devour the human sheep. There were none in the meadow now.

It was in the script, he knew. There was little he or anyone could do. The thought saddened him. He did not want to hurt anyone. He knew they were destroying the Earth; he knew they made him miserable. Jeremiah liked to see the best parts of things. And yet as he felt the bite of mid-November air on his ears (he forgot his hat, and hadn't realized he was cold until just then), he knew his life was a prison. Or a maze designed to confuse him, maybe. He could leave it all, he knew. Was he ready?

Things were happening regardless. On his way to the park Jeremiah saw the great chaos of traffic, of pedestrians wandering in distraction, swept away on a wave they could not see, the mechanics of which lay so far beyond their capacity to control or comprehend that they might as well ignore it and go with the mindless flow.

But Jeremiah's jeans were black, the legs were thirty-six inches wide, and he felt pretty awesome to be dressing however and doing whatever he damn well pleased. Jeremiah moved up and down a lot when he walked; he rolled or bounced a little with every step. It embarrassed him ordinarily. Today it felt good to walk on his toes. He noticed the natural feeling of it on the path out of the park to rejoin the party (Mary and Lea were watching the place), so he would walk home like a dinosaur. It was just what he felt.

He encountered a very ordinary-looking couple on the path along the meadow. Heading in the opposite direction, they took a good look at him and, indeed, looked horrified.

That was fine by him.

INTERLUDE III

"She *steals* from me," said his grandma.

His family ate with her every Friday night. The woman who lived with her would leave the apartment while they ate dinner.

"Mom, I thought you liked this one." His dad looked tired.

"*Before* she stole my watch and my necklace. Where's my necklace? Where's my watch?"

"Maybe you lost them, Bess. Maybe they fell behind the—"

"Laura, *please*," said his dad, jamming his palm at Jeremiah's mother. Then he turned back to Grandma, and asked if she'd looked under the bed or the couch.

"Maybe *you* stole them," she said.

Jeremiah, who had finished his dinner, had nothing to do but tease Rachel. His father warned him. When he started again his father grabbed his arm.

"You leave him alone," his grandma said.

His dad let go. "Yeah, right, Ma. He never does anything, I know."

"Why won't you tell me you love me?" They were in the kitchen. Jeremiah was helping his dad cook, and stood up on the stool to spin the lettuce on the counter. It was one of the things he was old enough to do. He had just turned four.

"Because you're mean," Jeremiah said. He did not stop, or look up.

"I'm not mean now, am I?"

He thought about it. "No."

"So why can't you love me when I'm nice?"

Jeremiah leaned on his arm for momentum. He wished his dad would disappear.

"It makes me sad. You know?"

He spun a few more times and stopped. The handle kept spinning, and his eyes followed.

"I'll love you when I'm five," he answered, buying time.

For the next eight years, what was left of his grandma would slowly disappear. The rest of her composure would go first. A year later, when he'd visit her with Jamilla, his grandma would call him a "hoodlum" and grab his arm and he would get pulled back and forth between her and Jamilla, who would yell, "Essie, let him go!" Next she would lose the use of her legs, then her arms and the rest of her body.

His father would hire extra help, two at a time, to keep her at home as long as he could. When she finally moved to the Morningside Jewish Home and Hospital, her forgetfulness wouldn't account for everything that disappeared from her apartment: antique jewelry, shelf ornaments, even a Persian rug that had been rolled up in the closet—all gone. So many helpers would come and go those years that there would be nowhere to start looking.

In the course of time even her family would disappear. His grandma's sisters and nephews and nieces would all stop visiting her. For his father they would bemoan her fate: the cruelty, the unfairness…she had been "so wonderful before," they "couldn't stand to see her." His father would stop visiting them, too, and so would Jeremiah.

Scary old ladies would crowd the hall of his grandma's floor whenever Jeremiah visited. No matter how quickly or quietly he stepped, the ones who could still walk would push up off their chairs; the rest would descend from their rooms. They would clap their hands and moan. Shocks of white and yellow hair; wrinkled arms would claw at Jeremiah and his sister. To reach his grandma's room they'd have to walk the row of toothless monsters. It was a lot like a haunted house but very bright and real (the smells made it much *too* real) and really no fun at all. Rachel would grab Jamilla's leg and Jeremiah would keep as close as he could without cravenly holding.

Seeing his grandma the way she'd become—silent, shrunken in her bed—would not be hard for him. He couldn't remember the time he'd spent with her before she got sick, when she took him to the park and was proud of his once curly, once much redder hair. The ghost of a woman he hardly remembered in the soft light of her room would only come in relief to the harsh hospital glare of the hall and the monsters outside. They would visit her every Friday at first, then twice a month, then once. Soon his dad stopped making them go. Jeremiah would never ask. He would never ask why they stopped. It would seem important to him only years later. That was when he would decide that changing, or even forgetting things he could remember but didn't like, would not be true, not even in fiction.

PART III

And if California slides into the ocean
like the mystics and statistics say it will
I predict this motel will be standing until I pay my bill

Warren Zevon

CHAPTER EIGHT
Birthright

I believe that for me life has ended and world history begun
—Theodore Herzl

January 2003

We arrived, battered from a ten-hour flight, at Ben Gurion International Airport, and suddenly we'd emerged somewhere between Tel Aviv and Jerusalem.

Tel-a-veev...

Jer-ooo-salem...

The names alone were an incantation conjuring ghosts of a youth I'd almost forgotten. But on this "Birthright" mission (for me it was part pilgrimage, part reconnaissance, part looking for a fight), youthful emotion would yield to a stronger, more mature, and critical mind.

And what a mind it was—a sharp, voracious intellect, whetted with months of *New York Times* editorials, *Harper's* features, Tony Judt essays in the *New York Review of Books*, and a tome by the omni-opinioned Tom Friedman to a savage blade that would slice through sentimentality and groupthink in one fell swoop.

Despite my parents, and CNN, and everything I knew about Israel from the sound bites and six-second video clips of carnage; despite what I might be expected to think, I hadn't really been afraid to emerge straight from the airport into a warzone bursting with gunshots, tanks, and combustible Arabs. The parking lot was just a parking lot, much like any I'd seen. Still, roughed up from the flight, dragging my duffle through sliding-glass doors to the column of three grim, tinted buses glaring down like Imperial Walkers, the ease of our Israeli "Madrichim" and security guards surprised me. They smiled and chatted with each other. Some of the friendlier guests talked to them.

The American hordes gathered by the imperial shuttles to claim our birthright. We were separated into three groups, one for each bus, and our tours would differ slightly. My group of twenty-something—in age and number—young Jewish American students and professionals were corralled in a circle, and made to hold hands and hop around chanting, "Achim! Achim! Achim, achim, achim! Simcha! Simcha! Simcha, simcha, simcha!" My first thought was that I alone found this absurd, like maybe they were laying it on kind of thick for a group of adults, young as we may have been. Everyone did have stupid smiles on their faces, but I smiled too.

Awkwardness aside, we seemed pretty conspicuous—a *jihadi*'s field day for the hidden sniper. And yet our guides, Yaniv and Shlomo, boldly conducted our stentorian cry of Jewish solidarity, publicly, out in the open air, in disputed lands full of Arabs. One was our bus driver. It was a detail I couldn't help noticing.

Our two guards stood at ease. Their rifles rested slung behind them. But their presence alone, or that of their guns, was unnerving. I locked eyes with the shorter one, a squat and stoic Israeli with a massive buzz-cut dome and a round, stubbled face. He was handsome in a brutish bulldog sort of way—sleek black eyebrows and dark brown eyes, severe and shifty like mine got. The guard would later earn a name, and Zaphir and I would become good friends. Now, the anonymous gunmen reminded me of the whole Zionist militant enterprise I was meant to abhor as the progressive, artsy-intellectual I conceived myself to be. Two years out of college, all puffed up on poststructuralist, post-nationalist, post-coherent theory, I had little use for tradition or tribal allegiance.

—

For most of the drive to Jerusalem I saw nothing biblical, ancient, or very pretty. It looked like lots of places I'd seen. I saw plains and hills, exurban sprawl, brown hints of desert. The dwellings that were visible from the road looked like nothing interesting, except in a few Arab villages, where houses stacked in precarious piles of three and four huddled around minarets stuck up like fingers aimed at God.

Though I hadn't expected heaven on earth any more than a greeting of mortar fire, I had hoped for more than what I saw. Despite myself I wanted something extraordinary, some grand, imposing relic or landscape evoking the magic and beauty of my heritage. I watched for something, anything to exhume memories of elementary school, of youth and pain, of God and the bittersweet pangs of nostalgia. I had begun to explore the past in writing. I had to remember what I could, to fill the celestial map with stars to navigate by—clear, crystalline, and fixed. So much was tangled up, I knew, in the memory of a dream of Israel.

But she had to impress me now, in the flesh. I wanted it right away and she couldn't deliver. Not even when we pulled over, filed off the bus, and gazed across the valley at the city I'd dreamt of as a boy. Even beholding the city under siege that summoned me across oceans and years of indifference, from a view that might have inspired awe, Jerusalem looked pretty, picturesque maybe, but nothing more. That evening we went en masse to the Wailing Wall. I donned my yarmulke, one of the cheap, thin black synthetic ones my mom must have "borrowed" from our synagogue years before to use on Passover. Crowds of black hats, black cloaks, black shawls, and somber earth-tone dresses gathered before the little great wall, all packed up front like checkers piled on the board.

Prayer was segregated here. Women prayed on the right behind a cordon; to the left, a regiment of black hats dominated the men's section. The hats belonged to both Haredim and Hassidim, though the distinction was lost on me then. At the time I thought all bearded, side-locked Jews in black were Hassids. In the years to come I would learn to identify the "more traditional" ultra-orthodox by their full but well-groomed beards and spiffy trench coats over expensive black suits; they covered their heads in black fedoras. The once-heretical, now established Hassids wore long cloaks and rounder black felt hats, or brown furry ones like flying saucers. The whole Martian ensemble was a throwback to some godforsaken eighteenth-century ghetto in Poland or Latvia.

The men of the more traditional sects were all well-groomed and dressed compared to the numerous devotees of the youngest, and still "controversial," offshoots of Hassidic mysticism. The Breslovers sang and danced a lot and wore only their tzitzim and white religious underwear with knit kippot. The Lubavitchers, or Chabads, whose men I'd learn to identify by their scraggly beards and threadbare suits, eschewed the fancy hats of their more traditional Hassidic forebears for shoddy, worn fedoras—no mark of class but a statement against vanity. These were austerity measures adopted by even the wealthiest Chabad men, while the women were often beautiful and dressed better than other Hassidic wives, which made no sense at all until I met some Chabad families. The wives all had, or wanted, or at least kept pace to spawn six to twelve little Mendels and Mushkies, and each would spawn six to twelve more, and what would be left of the rest of us?

None of this occurred to me then. I resented all varieties equally, and I could not tell them apart. These were the anachronisms on the subway in New York, lurking around the Diamond District or shaking lulafs at wayward Jews out on the piazza by the public library. They made me uncomfortable. Maybe they embarrassed me. I might have been ashamed to come from all that, to have ancestors who looked and dressed and lived like this. Maybe I felt judged.

But I watched them closely now, part scandalized and part mesmerized. I had never spent much time getting to know Brooklyn, even though I'd been living out there for a year. I'd never walked down Ocean Parkway and seen nothing but Jews in black costumes for literally miles. So now, as I watched these relics of my faith amassed in prayer, I saw the Jeremiad armies rising from the grave to Judgment.

I approached the wall and the fray of men in black thrusting against it. I walked with a sense of embarrassment, and thought of turning back, but despite the chorus of voices deterring me, some silent influence compelled me forward. Between a fedora and a fur saucer I found my spot. I placed a hand on a cool stone block worn smooth by the hands of millions of Jews exiled and scattered across the Earth. My hands could feel their hands. I felt their communion and rebirth in the old vibration of fear, shame, and sorrow transmuted to hope.

I said the first prayer that occurred, the only appropriate blessing I knew: "Shema Yisrael, Adonai eloheinu, Adonai echad." Then my forehead pressed against the Wall, the headstone of the Temple's Ghost, and the fist in my skull unclenched.

The yarmulke I wore that day meant nothing special before. It had been a small concession to a faith that claimed me in blood, yet was never quite mine, or for years I resisted its claim.

But the Wall had impressed me. Its ancient mass had stirred up more than expected. So as the sun set and we walked through the Muslim quarter of East Jerusalem, through alleyways, beneath passages likely accessible to people who might prefer that we walk somewhere else, in a group of fifty conspicuous Jews with a half-dozen armed escorts (two guards slung mini Uzis), the skullcap felt like part of a uniform. The danger I imagined we were in excited me. Beneath a steady walk I felt electric—fanatical almost. I was proud, intensely proud of the kippah I wore. I was proud not despite but because of the insult it meant.

But the Arabs paid little attention to us. An old woman, a shopkeeper with a moustache, a few toddlers glanced our way. The natives were used to these incursions.

—

It weighed on my mind the next morning: the guilt. Emotion had ambushed me with overwhelming force after only one day in Jerusalem. I had been exhausted from the flight, sleep deprived and delirious, clearly. Whatever the case, I had let down my guard, and it was a job for Tom Friedman.

Tom will set me straight, I thought, sitting down at a small table in the Dan Panorama Hotel lobby with my half-read copy of *From Beirut to Jerusalem*. The lobby bustled with young Jewish tourists, hundreds of us. We were mostly American, largely upper-middle class, and rich philanthropist Jews had paid for everyone to see Israel.

My reading was soon interrupted. It was Rivka, a girl in my group. We had flirted a little the night before. She sat down next to me with Etai, an Israeli with our group who was neither a leader nor a guard. A few like him went around with us so young American guests had young Israelis to experience. One of my roommates, Isaac Schwartz, would first experience Effrat, then Maya, for which our other roommate, Brad, and I would owe Isaac a steak dinner at Peter Luger to be paid up months later.

How did I like the book, Rivka was asking?

"It's good" I said. "He knows his stuff."

"I'm not sure how I feel about Tom Friedman. He's smart, but—"

"He's not just smart," I corrected. "He probably knows more about the region than any Westerner." I had the habit of making these remarkable, remarkably confident statements proving nothing so convincingly as my ignorance. It had nothing to do with Friedman, or his work; his was the only full-length book I had read on "the region," and I'd only read half.

"Lots of Westerners know a lot about the region" she said.

"Yeah, but this guy's different," I informed this Rivka. "Friedman spent twelve years living in Beirut."

She didn't seem convinced.

"I'm looking forward to Yad Vashem today."

"What's that?" I asked.

"The Holocaust museum" she said, like a question.

"Oh." Yeah, that would be a real party. "I just hope this trip doesn't turn out to be some propaganda tour," I added. "I hope we get a more balanced perspective of things, you know, at some point."

Silently, it was then that Rivka first concluded that I—this Jeremiah guy—was a jerk. Four years later we'd be married.

By the time we filed off the bus at Yad Vashem, the silence had spread through us all. Yaniv and Shlomo herded us through the gate like solemn sheep. We traversed the site to a garden with low wooden benches, and sat in a semicircle on the benches and the grass. Yaniv opened with some clichés about the Holocaust, the "unspeakable tragedy…never before seen, maybe, for all the history of mankind." He closed with an invocation to us to talk about someone we knew, a family member or friend who had suffered and survived. Two or three people told stories about their grandparents.

Everyone's face became a mask of vacant gravity—boredom and discomfort thinly veiled. We knew we were meant to feel sad and ruminative but couldn't quite get there. The cud was too chewed up, too often regurgitated and swallowed again in years of Hebrew school. We were actors in a tired script seeking our motivation.

Being there felt forced. I resented feeling obligated to put on a grim face as soon as we crossed the gate. It was like we were expected to feel this grief beyond words, whether or not we could, like our feelings had been decided for us. And it mattered little how many trees and flowers were planted to liven things up, or how elegantly minimal the buildings and sculptures were. By some unspoken code the nuance of living emotion felt vulgar here, in this manicured mass grave—a campus for the dead. You almost felt ashamed for living.

We began at the Hall of Names, a dark room hollowed out from an underground cavern. The room was a planetarium of souls. It glowed dimly with star-like, infinitesimal pinpricks of light. It was a trick of invisible mirrors. The stars were a single candle flame reflected ad nauseam to approximate the 1.5 million Jewish children murdered in Europe. Each name was intoned in disembodied male and female voices revolving endlessly. So if you were trapped underground in the cave forever, you'd just keep hearing the same names over and over and over again.

It might have had an impact then. That might have been appropriate for the German artists who inspired the Hall. Why were *we* here, though?

Next we stopped in front of two large friezes in white marble. Both were monuments to murdered Jews. The first depicted a crowd of them lined up and led to the camps; the second was a heroic biblical scene dedicated specifically to those who died fighting in the Warsaw Ghetto Uprising.

Shlomo explained that for many years after the war, and then after Israel declared independence, Israelis preferred never to mention the Holocaust. They were ashamed of it, totally racked with guilt from the violence and trauma "we" had suffered. It embarrassed Jews and stole their dignity and they repressed it. Israelis once saw the Jews of the Holocaust as cowards and fools who died without a fight, said Shlomo, like lambs led to slaughter. They only discussed the Holocaust, if ever, to brandish the brave rebels of Warsaw.

That was how it was in the years before Yad Vashem. The center was built in part to rectify the image of Holocaust victims and survivors. The founders sought to portray them in a different light. And the perception began to shift. Cowards and fools became sufferers and proud survivors of a terrible fate that was always beyond their control. The center revealed just how little Jews could have done to defend themselves, with no homeland, in a world that devised and ignored their plight. Soon it became important—all important—to remember.

And remember we did. In light of the holocaust, claimed Shlomo, one could understand Israel's present-day "focus on security."

"But isn't it dangerous," I interrupted, "to talk about what Israel is doing today in reference to the Holocaust?" I heard the first scoff somewhere to my right.

"How do you mean?" said Shlomo. "What is Israel doing?"

"The occupation." Another scoff. I chose to ignore it again.

"I said nothing about an occupation. I was speaking of the Holocaust in relation to the importance of security for Israelis."

"But that doesn't excuse the oppression of an entire nationality."

"What are you talking about?"

I turned finally to confront my heckler. It was Nadya, the shrill and boisterous newly indoctrinated Orthodox Jewess—a *ba'al teshuva,* or *ba'alat* in the feminine. One always heard her voice above all others on the bus. Wherever we traveled, Nadya brought her opinions. The day before, in the old city, outside some ancient church, apropos of some historical factoid on Jesus courtesy of Shlomo, Nadya had considered it her religious duty to alert us all to the dearth of hard historical proof that The Christ ever existed. Nadya had been observant for less than a year and already refused handshakes from men. She was from Oak Park, Illinois, and talked like a Crown Heights Yenta.

"What do you mean?" she repeated. "Israelis get sad about the Holocaust and then go and kill Palestinians? Is that what you're saying?"

I paused for composure. "No."

"Then why won't you say what you mean?"

"Because," I said, "I don't respond to hostility."

As the group dispersed and moved to the next exhibit, Kyle, a long-haired, squinting apparatchik, honored me with a complicitous sneer reserved for kindred spirits. The frowsy Ché in frayed t-shirts would soon replace me in the role of group conscience. He would come ready, locked and loaded for each lecture, spraying Chomsky and Pinochet all over the room like wild bullets.

I caught Rivka's eye. Her look was neutral—the slight

tensing of lips, a subtle lift of brows. I could not read it—yet, anyway. I did not know her pale pretty face and its six million permutations. I'd never watched it shift in the turbulence of her heart from love to loathing, from hope to despair and back. With the benefit of hindsight, though, I guess what registered on Rivka's face right then was something like confirmation.

The walls of the next room were covered in black-and-white photos of starving Jews—men, women, and children like pale Somalians. Their cheeks were concave; their eyes were too big for their skulls. A group of soldiers toured the room, each heavily armed. They listened to a Hebrew lecture by a woman in civilian clothes, a guide from the center.

I heard someone cry out, and turned to locate the despair. An Israeli girl in the room with us had become distraught. This stunning dark girl in a brown headscarf collapsed on the floor at her parents' feet, and sobbed like she'd been in the camps herself, or she'd lost the same parents there.

The force of her grief struck me—what could the Holocaust mean to her? Maybe she had a relative who suffered, survived, and died years later. Did the spirit of her beloved departed touch her then? Maybe her soul was gentle enough to mourn the suffering of all souls, even those she never knew, or not in this life, on this Earth.

Most of the seats were taken once I flicked my cigarette and climbed the steps up onto the bus. I cast an imposing glance down the aisle at everyone and no one at all, avoiding eye contact, and found two empty seats together a few rows back. I sat and waited silently. Rivka may have been the last to board. She took a few steps toward the first empty seat, next to me, and sat.

"Hi," she said, not pointed but matter-of-fact. "Hope you don't mind if I sit here."

"Why would I mind?"

She looked away, glanced furtively into space.

As the bus pulled away from Yad Vashem, I asked her what she thought.

"I don't know if I liked it," she said, "but I thought it was beautiful. Totally devastating, obviously. You?"

"Parts of it were moving," I said. "For me."

"What was your favorite? The children's memorial?"

"The room with the stars? That was nice. Artful, I guess. But no, that room didn't quite hit home."

"Really? I loved it," she said. "So, what was it then? What got through to you?"

A scratching burst over the speakers. The sound was annoyingly familiar, and I knew without looking that Shlomo was "shaving" his salt-and-pepper stubble with the microphone and broadcasting the noise for everyone. He followed with one of his signature awful, idiomatic Israeli jokes, which he butchered more in translation. It was like the official sign we'd left Holocaust land. Our leader's antics signaled we could breathe a sigh and resume our wacky Promised Land adventures. Finally, really driving it home, he announced we would stop at a mall.

"You know what it is, maybe?" I said, cutting carefully to the core. "These places, Holocaust museums and memorials, or whatever…it's like…you know they're really important in some ways, I guess. I mean, the Holocaust was terrible and all, and it should be remembered. History is important," I conceded humbly. "But is the past everything? What about today? Right now? Is the Holocaust really all that important to what's going on in the world today?"

I'd had Israel, the occupation, and conflict on the brain when I asked the question. But Rivka took me literally. She talked about anti-Semitism, its resurgence around the world with the second Intifada. It was getting worse, she insisted, and not just in the Arab world and in Europe, but America too.

"In America? Really?" I asked her if she'd had any experience with ant-Semitism back home. She talked about her college, the large and frequent anti-Israel protests among the students, the professors signing petitions to "boycott" the Jewish State. I was about to explain that criticism of Israel wasn't anti-Semitic, or not necessarily, but Rivka had more to say.

"I was on the subway once when this big, goofy-looking Hassidish guy came in the door from the next car. He was marching down the aisle all nervous and panicky." Rivka demonstrated with her eyebrows; her arms jerked out to the side all clenched. I laughed. "I think he might have been a little slow or something," she continued. "Not retarded maybe, but probably kinda slow, or a little Asperger-y, you know. And he had this really sweet, scared look in his face, and I had this intense protective feeling toward him—like he needed my help."

She was looking out toward the front of the bus. There was something about this girl. I liked listening.

"Then the door he'd just come through opened again and this Muslim walked into to our car."

"How'd you know he was Muslim?"

"He had a beard and of those hats and he was holding a Koran."

I was satisfied.

"So the Jewish guy turns around and says, 'Stop following me! Why are you following me?'" She deepened and raised her voice to channel the frightened Hassid.

My heart beat suddenly fast—the old rage I would need to suppress.

"When the Jewish guy got to the door for the next car over, the Muslim attacked him. He smashed him right in the face." She swung back her arm.

"So what happened?"

"Some people on the train jumped the guy and wrestled him down. I looked over at the Hassid and saw he was bleeding. There was blood all down the side of face." She stuck out her cheek and traced the invisible bloodline with two fingers. "I hadn't seen him holding it, but the Muslim guy had a hammer. I saw it on the floor all bloody."

My mouth had literally dropped.

"I went over to this poor guy and helped him off the train and sat him down on a bench."

"So it stopped? The train?"

"Yeah, the conductor stopped it in the station." It was somewhere in Brooklyn.

"And what happened to the other guy?" I said. "The Muslim?"

"I sat there with the Yeshiva boy and waited for the police. They took the other guy away and I stayed with him until the paramedics came for him. And he kept saying, 'Why was that man following me? Why did he hit me?' I didn't know what to say. He seemed so sweet and helpless."

My throat was sore.

At the entrance to the mall we waited in line to pass through a buffer zone of soldiers with assault rifles and a metal detector. My heart, which had started to race with Rivka's story, still pounded a bit. I imagined going through all this two or three times every day. I wondered why, after 9/11, I still almost never did.

The next morning at Independence Hall in Herzliya, a suburb of Tel Aviv, a man named Moshe or Avram greeted us. He was shortish, stockyish, kind of swarthy. He had curly black hair and the kind of eyebrows you noticed right away. Our host was animated. He smiled and gesticulated with dramatic vigor. This would be fun. Now we'd get a history lesson from an authentic Israeli cartoon: Moshe or Avram the Wild and Crazy Israeli Tour Guide.

Our program began in a small room with a projection screen. Our host played a short propaganda film of black-and-white photo montages of early Jewish settlers in Ottoman and British Palestine; post-Independence footage of new Israelis draining swamps and magically conjuring trees and lush green fields from brown desert; cheerful narration from an American English generic male voice in circa 1950s documentary inflections over ancient upbeat electro grooves, reminiscent of the scores composed for Atari games. The film might have been made in the seventies. A stilted phrase here, a cheesy melodic flourish there made us laugh. Our host sat near the screen to the side. I saw him in profile. He showed no sign of getting the joke, though he didn't look offended. It may have been that he heard it five times a day.

After the film we followed him to a larger room with a bigger screen and a slide projector. He stood at the front of the room. The group with our leaders and guards sat in chairs facing him. He opened with a riff on Theodore Herzl, a man he admired, clearly. He spoke about anti-Semitism in Herzl's time and the Dreyfus affair. A journalist in Paris, in the land of the French Revolution (the great "Liberation"), Herzl witnessed mobs of French shouting "Death to the Jews." Until then he had been an assimilationist.

Though Jews had mixed in Europe in large numbers, marrying and living among gentiles, many remained "ghettoized." Some believed the hatred directed at European Jewry was a symptom of self-segregation. If we weren't so different—so tribal—if Jews didn't wear our beards so long or grow side locks or dress like we were always off to a funeral, normal humans would see that Jews were human, too.

Herzl and his family, secular, socialist Jews, had left the ghetto. But then—in the land of Liberty and Enlightened Rationalism—so had Colonel Dreyfus.

He concluded that anti-Semitism was inherent in human nature. It was inevitable. Our persecution was rooted in our existence and in theirs. No matter what we did, no matter how well we succeeded in blending with our host culture, for them we would remain a foreign entity to isolate, uproot, and cleanse.

So Herzl believed we needed a home, said our host. We needed a nation where Jews would be the majority. And where better than the home that once belonged to us, the Diaspora that disbanded and scattered the earth to suffer, and suffer more injustice everywhere? And now, with pogroms like brush fires burning through Europe, it was urgent for Jews to reunite. We stood a chance in numbers alone, in a home to protect. We needed an old-new home together again, and apart from the world.

Or else, wrote Herzl in his journals, the "windows of Jewish homes" would "turn to broken glass." He wrote it more than fifty years before Kristallnacht.

"Adolph Hitler," said our host, "had a mistress, Eva, who everyone said he adored. He also had a dog, Blondi." This earned a few laughs.

"At the end of the war, when the Russians were closing in on Hitler in his bunker, he married Eva, then threw a party with his staff. During his party Hitler reminisced on the good old days when the Nazis were steamrolling over Europe. He told his secretary he knew the war was lost, and he swore he would never allow himself to be captured. The next day, when the gunshots and the explosions were all around him, Hitler knew his time had come. He gave a poison capsule to his bride—at her request. He gave one capsule also to his dog. He couldn't stand the thought of Blondi being a prisoner of the Russians and Jews. So he took care of Blondi last before he shot himself.

"Sounds like a pretty nice guy after all, this Hitler. No? Before he blew out his brains he stopped and shook hands with all of his staff, even the peons he never knew, and he said goodbye to his personal secretaries, Gerda and Gertrude. Both of Hitler's secretaries said he was wonderful—always generous and kind to them, like a nice uncle. Uncle Adolph."

And with that our host earned his first laugh from me.

"His last thoughts were for his staff," he continued, "for his bride, and finally for his dog. Even Hitler had love in his heart. So we have to look closely now, young ladies and gentlemen, you see? The devil won't always wear horns."

He paused emphatically.

"The British had been restricting Jewish immigration into Palestine all along, years after declaring Jews' national rights. During the war, and even after the war, even after the Holocaust, the British government refused to end the restriction. There were hundreds and thousands of survivors, many who had been in the camps. They had nowhere to go when the war ended. Many wanted to come here and the British refused them.

"And what was done with these Jews—these survivors? Does anyone know where the British sent them?"

"Cyprus?" someone said.

"That's right. Cyprus." He said it like something about the place or its name was outrageous. My vague picture of Cyprus was of an exotic island somewhere in the Mediterranean. The image involved the faint outline of arid cliffs, a white-sand beach and the pastel shadows of palms. Certainly, it seemed, there were far worse places to land.

"And where were they kept in Cyprus?" he asked.

"Camps?" the same girl volunteered.

"Camps!" he said with a smile. "That's right. The British sent the Jews to camps. Straight from Auschwitz. Boatfuls of Jews seeking refuge were turned away at the port in Palestine and sent to Cyprus—tens of thousands in hot and filthy refugee camps. They were detained like criminals, with barbed wire fences and everything. And many more Jews died there. They survived the gas chamber to die of hunger and diseases. They died waiting."

He clicked the remote; the slide shifted to a split-screen image of said camps and fences. This man had my attention now. He was hitting the notes.

"Now, for some reason this upset the Jews. Jewish militias in Palestine were fighting an insurgency against the British for years, and when the war ended and the death camps opened for the world to see and survivors of the Holocaust were sent back to camps, the resistance intensified. Menachem Begin's Irgun militia bombed the King David Hotel in Yerushalaim. At this time the British occupying authority used the hotel as a base of operations.

"Begin warned the British the day before the attack. The Irgun called in the threat, told them exactly what they would do, and warned them to evacuate the building. But the British ignored it. They didn't believe these upstart desert Hebrews could pull off something like this. They never thought the Jews could get past the British security.

"They did, and ninety people were killed—some of them Jews who worked for the British. I'm not saying Begin should have done it, but he did warn them. That's a better deal than you will ever get from Hamas."

Our host continued his lecture with the British short on funds and caught between Jewish and Arab demands, when in February 1947 the Attlee government in Great Britain declared its mandate in Palestine "unworkable." The British referred the matter to the fledgling UN, which formed the Special Committee on Palestine. The UN committee, in a display of short-lived sympathy for the Jews after the Holocaust, recommended an end to the British mandate and the partitioning of the land.

The screen now projected a map of the Jewish State and Palestine as envisioned in the UN's partition plan, a series of red and blue chunks and slivers interspersed.

"Here's the first map of Israel." He pointed on the projector at a blue chunk in the southeastern area of Israel's current map, by far the largest portion accorded to the Jews. "Does anyone know what this is?"

"Desert," said someone.

"Right," he said. "The Negev. Thank you, United Nations!" People laughed. "And did the Jews complain?" He paused, then answering his own question: "The day the UN passed Resolution 181 recognizing Jewish nationhood, Jews in Israel and across the world were dancing in the street. They were dancing. In America, too. It's true—you can ask your grandparents. They'll remember it.

"And we wasted none of it. Israelis and Jews from all over the world came to cultivate the desert—they built farms in the Negev—and to drain the swamps. Those people in the film, you know, with the funny music?" A few chuckles. "Well, people actually did these things. They gave their sweat and blood for this land. Yerushalaim was decaying. Muslim holy land, ha! They neglected it for centuries. It was a backwater of the Ottoman Empire, totally in decay. And look at it now. Look what we've made it, again.

"And the Arabs? Were they satisfied? Was it enough for them to have half of what remained of the land of Israel to call Palestine? The half that had the trees and the water?"

I knew this was the type of question he'd ask to answer.

"After the UN passed its resolution recognizing a Jewish state, the League of Arab States met and passed its own resolution: 'This will be a war of extermination and a momentous massacre which will be spoken of like the Mongolian massacres and the Crusades.' That was Azzam Pasha, the Arab League secretary-general, threatening genocide against Jews. Haj Amin al-Husseini—remember Hitler's Mufti?—Haj Amin issued a fatwa: 'I declare a holy war, my Muslim brothers! Murder the Jews! Murder them all!'

"The Arabs like to play the victims today, but not then. Oh no. They had no need for this, or so they thought. A few months later, when they attacked the Jews and started the Independence War, Jamal Husseini, a spokesman for the Mufti, delivered a message before the UN Security Council: 'The representative of the Jewish Agency told us yesterday that they were not the attackers, that the Arabs had begun the fighting. We did not deny this. We told the whole world that we were going to fight.'"

With a grin he lowered the sheet he quoted from.

"The Arabs had forty tanks to our one. They had two hundred armored vehicles; we had two. They had over seventy warplanes. We didn't have a single plane, not at first. A man named Montgomery, commander of the Allied Forces in Africa and Europe in World War II, predicted the Jews would be slaughtered in two weeks.

"America didn't help us then. No, no. Truman told Ben-Gurion he was crazy. He said forget it. Do not declare independence now, he said, it would be suicide for the Jews. Wait, he said, till the Jews are stronger. Truman offered him no weapons to discourage Ben-Gurion.

"But some Arab forces had already begun to attack, and Ben-Gurion was determined, and tired of waiting. So on the fourteenth of May, 1948, the day when the British were leaving, he called the Jewish leaders together in this building we are in right now to declare independence. And talk about chutz-*pah*—he did it before the British had gone. Ben-Gurion declared independence before the Great British Empire left.

"The Arabs reacted immediately, of course. The riots got bigger, and soon it became a full-on war when the Arab armies invaded Israel. The invading forces included soldiers from Syria, Lebanon, Egypt, Iraq, Transjordan, Yemen, and Saudi Arabia." His fingers counted each name. "Seven. It was fifty or sixty thousand Jews against seven Arab nations—eight, including the Palestinians. Ariel Sharon was a platoon commander at the time. He was injured at Latrun in a battle which Israel lost, and his men carried him several kilometers to safety. Keep in mind it was back when this was still possible."

The room laughed. I was starting to like this guy. I had started agreeing with him, or wanting to be convinced.

"You should see the guns these soldiers used in the Independence War. Old wooden rifles, old even then. Antiques. You, hold up your gun."

Zaphir the security guard held out his rifle. Everyone in the room now looked at the old wooden gun. It looked like one of the rifles from a booth at the county fair, where you shot lasers at stuffed animals.

"What issue is this?" said the host. "I think this one is the model after the Independence War, right?"

"It's the same."

"The same? You are joking! The same?"

Zaphir nodded.

"This gun is completely useless!" Our host was now ecstatic. "You couldn't shoot a house with this gun!"

The room was erupting. The guards' rifles had been an ongoing joke.

"Are you sure it will fire? You would need to smash it on

someone's head." He looked back at the rest of us as though to move on, but then, encouraged by all the laughter, turned back to Zaphir: "You would need to throw it at the terrorist! But you see the point now, yes?"

The laughter stopped.

"The world is totally convinced that Israel is this colonial monster—we'll stop at nothing until we've conquered all the lands of Greater Israel. Maybe we'll role our tanks into Damascus? Or Baghdad?

"Israel is a tiny country. We are surrounded by neighbors who despise us. They don't want peace with the Jews. Please, don't fool yourselves. We have something that is theirs and they want it back—everything. For the Jews they leave not even the desert, only the floor of the Mediterranean Sea.

"And I hear people speak with this incredible passion about the Palestinians and their heroic struggles for freedom—for a home. Not just Arabs; Jews, and Israelis even. A girl from another group last week—they were Jews from New Zealand— and this woman answered me almost in tears. Her voice was shaking for the Palestinians and their home."

He stopped mid-pace, turned forward.

"What about our home? Must Jews alone be homeless? Should we go back to the Arab nations that banished us? Back to Auschwitz?"

He turned, started pacing again. The room was electric in silence.

"Young people in Israel today are spoiled." His tone relaxed from the fever pitch it had built. "They finish the army, and afterward they travel to places like India or Thailand. And if they get in trouble for something they go crying to the Israeli embassy. This never existed before. Don't you see? There was no embassy for Jews during the Spanish Inquisition, or in nineteenth-century France, or during the Holocaust. So while you are here, remember—please. This is not some exotic getaway like Thailand or India. This is your home."

And I knew he was right.

We all rose once more, and finally entered the historic Hall. The auditorium had high ceilings. A gallery of seats faced a long table, with a middle chair between five or six seats on each flank. The middle chair, raised on a podium, was where Ben-Gurion sat that day among the founders, elevated among the architects of the modern State. On the wall behind the table a curtain hung between two long, slender blue and white flags stretching the height of the wall, and also between the flags, on the curtain, directly above Ben-Gurion's seat, hung a large, bearded portrait of the man himself, the founders' founder, Ted Herzl.

The group all sat in the gallery. Our host played a recording from the room we were now in, slightly below ground, where the Jews had gathered to secure themselves against the threat of bombs. Above the old crackling Ben-Gurion's actual voice read the proclamation. Our host seemed genuinely moved, in awe, which said a lot considering how many hundreds of times he'd heard the recording—at least once every day. There was deep respect and reverence in his voice when, after letting the Hebrew run for a line or two, he followed in English:

> The Land of Israel was the birthplace of the Jewish people.
> Here their spiritual, religious, and political identity was shaped.
> Here they first attained to statehood,
> created cultural values of national and universal significance
> and gave to the world the eternal Book of Books.
> After being forcibly exiled from their land,
> the people kept faith with it throughout their dispersion
> and never ceased to pray and hope for their return to it
> for the restoration of their political freedom.

It went on for a while, got more technical and covered much of the speech our host had given.

Finally, "Placing our trust in the Almighty, we affix our signatures to this proclamation, at this session of the provisional Council of State, on the soil of the Homeland, in the city of Tel Aviv, on this Sabbath eve, the fifth day of Iyar, 5708 (May 14, 1948)."

Then Ben-Gurion stopped and we heard the triumphant, pain-filled groans of the living ghosts who sat that day where we now sat, in the same gallery of the same hall. And the host said to everyone, "*Please*, I'll ask it respectfully. Please rise for the Hatikva."

The sad, familiar melody rose up on the tape from the ghost of an old brass band. It had none of the words, just the melody, but I sang the words in my head. It reminded me of elementary school, when the song I was hearing now was the most beautiful and mysterious and familiar song I knew, and although I could sing all the words I never understood them. At Hebrew school they never really teach you Hebrew.

We would continue an amazing tour. We would hear lectures from journalists, members of the Knesset and a former ambassador to the UN. We would drive up to the Golan Heights and gaze over the Lebanese border at yellow Hezbollah flags. We'd hike in the desert, climb Masada at dawn, and drive to look out over the vast crater of Mitzpe Ramon. We would walk through Safed and sit in the preserved synagogues of sixteenth-century Kabalistic rabbis and dance on Shabbos at a Carlebach Shul in Jerusalem. Ehud Ya'ari, "Arab Affairs Expert" for Israel's Channel 5, would deliver a lecture to us in a conference room of the Dan Panorama Jerusalem on how the Iraq War was inevitable and imminent and why it would be a good thing— good for Israel, for America, and for the whole world, even Iraq. With Saddam gone, Israel would lose an existential threat on its western flank. The settlement blocks, which acted as a buffer zone from the Arabs, would no longer be so important. Which would clear the way for strategic separation from Palestine, for negotiations with the PA, for a ceasefire and a treaty for lasting historic peace (the Iraqis would cheer allied forces as liberators). I was convinced. I would go on to support the war vocally and, indeed, I would vote for George W. Bush.

Rivka and I would kiss at a concert hidden in a maze of cobblestone alleys near the Old City. She would demur at first; she'd say I didn't want any of her. She was crazy: she wanted to get married and raise lots of Jewish babies. Me too.

Back in New York we would date for four years. We would dream about living in Israel one day, a year or so to start; maybe we'd conceive to birth our child in Eretz Yisrael. It would be a big Jewish wedding with lots of family and friends, bursting in laughter and joyous tears, in song and dance and well-earned sighs. A rich philanthropist Jew would pay for our honeymoon in St. Martins: we met on Birthright. Within months we would separate and divorce.

I'm not sure how to feel about everything. Not yet. I'm tired of explaining some things so I talk about others instead. Everything makes a certain kind of sense, rest assured.

I think it was Brad Pitt who once said to Angelina Jolie, "I guess that's what happens in the end, you start thinking about the beginning" (he said it in *Mr. and Mrs. Smith*). I for one go back to Independence Hall—to the Hatikva. Hearing that melody there, just then, was enough to change everything. Things would have gone different. It's just one of those feelings.

CHAPTER NINE
Reparations

"So now that I'm about to get married and, you know, start my own family soon…"

We'd ordered our dinner; the waiter was gone. I looked my father in the eye. My words were an accusation, like he was to blame for starting ours.

"I've been thinking about the responsibilities that come with all that—with kids especially. And when I think back on my childhood, and on some of the things you did, and as I come to realize more and more how those things affected me, I worry. I worry about being a father and making the same mistakes you made. I think of the way you made me feel growing up, and I hope, and I pray sometimes…"

The nod to God was a jab at him.

"I pray that I never put any child of mine through anything like that because of my miserable temper, which I got from you, clearly."

I paused to let it sink in.

"And you know, notwithstanding the fights we still have sometimes, I think we've learned to get along pretty well. And I appreciate all you've done for me in recent years, and always. And though I've struggled through a bunch of, um, *rough patches*…and maybe because I've ended up in a good place—"

"Not ended," he interrupted. It was the first he'd spoken in minutes.

"What?" I said.

"You're in a good place now," he said. "You haven't ended anywhere."

I absorbed it.

"Why are we having this talk here?" He scanned the interior of the neighborhood bistro. "Why now?"

"Because we've never had it before." I said it like I'd expected him to start. "So like I was saying, since now I'm no longer *just* a series of disappointments for you…"

He flinched. "I wonder whether you're inclined to overlook all those times in the past when you were shouting at me and smacking me around. Like maybe it's easy for you to forget all that stuff. Maybe you just kinda shrug it off, you know, like yesterday's news."

He shook his head. "You know what my memory's like."

He was always very impressed with his memory.

"Well, one curse that comes with the gift of a perfect memory is the inability to forget. So I remember all the good stuff, and all the bad stuff, too."

"Really? So tell me, do any specific incidents spring to mind? Like just off the top of your head?"

He paused, looked up, then down at his hands on the table. If he spoke or prepared to speak his eyes rarely met mine. It had always bothered me.

"I most often recall one incident…at Punta Brava." Our eyes met.

"On the beach."

"Right. But though I remember attacking you, that wasn't what bothered me most about that incident afterward. You know, you were a big seventeen-year-old boy. What I did to your sister was inexcusable."

"You don't say."

A pained expression took hold of his face again.

"How about when I was three, and you were scaring the piss out of me, literally? Or when I was eight, and we were in San Francisco?"

What was it about those fucking vacations?

"At the Exploratorium? Remember when Rachel and I were fighting over turns at some hands-on exhibit—you know, those stupid little magnets on strings that hook onto hanging cylinders? Then, with the wisdom of Solomon, you came to resolve the dispute by punching me in the stomach? From whatever you'd seen in three seconds, you decided I was to blame."

It was never quite clear how he chose who to hit.

"I remember being totally winded, doubled over in pain, and some good Samaritan coming up and calling you out and embarrassing you, and me too, of course, in front of all those people. Remember that? And you started cursing and threatening the guy like the tough guy you think you are, but you did nothing because you were caught with your righteous pants down. And you were ashamed. It was obvious. But that never stopped you."

"Okay," he cut in. "I'm not saying I never hurt you. I remember things when you were younger, too. I'm just saying that a seventeen-year-old boy and a fourteen-year-old girl are two different things."

"Let's not get dizzy splitting hairs. The point is, have you ever thought maybe things might have been a bit easier, like for *me*, if you'd done things differently? You know, you were always on my ass about everything, but did you ever think maybe the problem was you? Just a little?"

He took a deep breath. "After you had your trouble at Johnston that first semester, and then back home—you know? With the drugs and everything?"

Yes, I knew.

"I blamed myself completely then. I thought it was all my fault, that I'd screwed you up."

He looked at me. He looked away.

"And that's when I started to make what I believe has been a successful effort to control my temper with you and your sisters."

"I'll give you that. It's also possible that what motivated you to control your temper with me specifically was, as you say, I was getting older, and stronger, and if you kept trying to push me around maybe soon you'd have gotten your old ass kicked."

He grinned, rolled his eyes. "Come on?"

My eyes dared him.

"I'm sure you could kick my ass, Jeremiah."

He did not sound sure enough.

"But I don't think that's why I stopped. Maybe I brutalized you kids."

"That's your word. You used it, not me. Remember that."

"All right, I said it: brutalize. And maybe I did, but I also worked hard to change. And I also seem to recall you having fun as a kid. I remember taking you to all these places, and loving you very much, and I remember times when you seemed to be happy."

"Yes, of course. And I'm grateful for all of that."

"Forget being grateful. Weren't you happy, though? Sometimes?"

"Yes. Sometimes I was," I said. "It was almost like having two lives. Or two dads."

A silence passed between us.

"Jair, I don't expect you to understand what I went through when your grandma got sick. It was like she was losing her mind, and so was I. We were dying together."

He took a sip of water.

"And I thought about killing myself, every day for a while. And I thought about killing her, too. I decided it was up to me to end her suffering, and mine. These elaborate fantasies would play over and over again in my mind of killing my mother, then killing myself, and leaving you an orphan. And that was key— that I'd leave you an orphan. Since my mom was an orphan."

My grandmother's father died before she was born, and her mother in childbirth, which made her a "perfect orphan," as my dad liked to brag. An aunt brought her from Austria to America when she was two.

"The symbolism of it," he said. "You know? The symmetry."

I understood more than I liked.

"So why didn't you?"

"What?"

"Leave me an orphan."

He looked up and away. "Eventually I started therapy. And that really saved my life. It was a time when I got to focus on me alone. I could forget all about Grandma, and Mommy, and you, and just talk about me for an hour.

"But there was an incident first. I was at the apartment one day, home early from work. You must have been at nursery school because I remember being home alone with Rachel, and Jamilla was there, too. Rachel was still a baby. I remember it being her first birthday…that's right. I left work early that day to cook for the party. And Jamilla brought Rachel out, and she'd dressed her up all nice and pretty in this little white dress, and fixed up her hair in little bows and braids. And it occurred to me then how long it had been since I'd felt any emotion at all for my baby daughter. Your grandma was diagnosed just a few days after Rachel was born, which is when I checked out emotionally. The only real joy I'd ever felt in connection with her occurred on the day she was born, and even then it was obvious something was wrong with your grandma. And of course, I was already worried.

"So a full year had passed, and I realized that day I had missed the first year of my daughter's life. And I started crying. I just held her and sobbed."

Another sip.

"That's when I decided to talk to someone."

I nodded. The waiter brought two glasses of Chardonnay. He left.

"So why were you still such a prick for years? I mean, you softened up some. But what about all those years through Havarim and Riverbrook? What about the abuse I took for my grades and being fat? And what about Punta Brava?"

"At Punta Brava, Jair, you have to understand—I thought

you and Rachel were dead. I thought you had wandered off the resort and been robbed and murdered. For two hours."

"See, that's where your perfect memory seems to falter. We were eleven minutes late."

His eyebrows raised again. "I remember it being two hours."

"You remember wrong."

"I really don't think so."

A brief silence.

"But anyway," he said, "I was sure you were dead and I panicked."

"But why? Why would you assume that? Couldn't you have guessed we were stupid teenagers? You know, just fucking around? What's the matter with you? Why do you have to assume the worst? *Always*?"

He drained his water. His head turned every direction but mine. "Look, Jair. There really are no rules for this stuff. I mean, you think you've had parents, and you've learned from their mistakes and all that. And you do, sometimes, in certain ways. But then you have your own kids, and you really have no idea what to expect or how to handle certain things. And I know I've made lots of mistakes. I see it now. I started seeing it years ago. And no, I'm still not perfect, but I've tried. I've tried hard to be a good father to you and the girls. What else can I do?"

"Has it ever once occurred to you," I said, "to apologize?"

He looked up at me then. The steel cage of his body relaxed and there was pleading in his voice when my father said, "I'm *sorry*, Jeremiah."

POSTSCRIPT

One Sunday afternoon Jeremiah went shopping with his dad, as they had most weekends for over two years. They pushed through the crowd at Fairway. Jeremiah had grown too big to sit in the cart. The sawdust smell of the floor mixed at different counters with fresh bread, ground coffee, smoked fish…

Like always his dad cracked walnuts between his palms for Jeremiah to eat. As usual he got to choose the best fruits and avocadoes. He also got to pick two flavors of ice cream, and when he asked if they could have waffles or blintzes for Sunday brunch, his dad bought both. Jeremiah missed his seat in the cart.

Behind the counter Dave the cheese man was excited to see Jeremiah. He gave him free slices of Swiss. He made a big deal—though a little less than he used to make—over Jeremiah's curly red hair. It really wasn't so curly, not anymore, and it was a little less red.

Across the street, at Nevada, the butcher gave him his usual salami and bologna treats. He seemed very impressed by how much Jeremiah had grown. His father smiled at him while he talked to the butcher. He often smiled when Jeremiah talked. He'd said his first word at seven months. His dad liked to tell the story of how Jeremiah sat in his mom's lap while his dad took their picture, and after the flash Jeremiah pointed up at the spot in the air where the bright white light had been and he said "moon." And ever since his dad liked to show him off. He knew it made his dad proud, watching him talk to people about things his dad had taught him: the tallest skyscrapers, the highest mountains, the seven ancient Wonders of the World, and the gibbous moon (when you could almost see the whole thing, and you couldn't tell something was missing unless you looked close). Jeremiah liked to show off. He loved it when his dad was there.

Jeremiah left the butcher on his dad's shoulders.

"Soon you'll be too big for this," said his dad.

"When?" Not too soon, he hoped.

"We'll see. When you're five, maybe."

Jeremiah said nothing.

"Don't worry. You can ride up there as long as you want."

They took a detour through the park. Jeremiah asked his dad to carry him in his arms, like when he was smaller. His dad said okay, for a little bit, and slid Jeremiah down from his shoulders into the arms that were free, since the groceries were being delivered. It was fall; the trees were bright domes of orange, purple, yellow, and red. On the ground the leaves were mixed in rainbow piles and scattered. A few people jogged, biked, or skated past them. Holding Jeremiah under his arms and legs, his dad walked with him along the road to the Sheep Meadow. When Jeremiah asked they turned away from the road leading out of the park toward home, and followed the path around the big green field surrounded by distant towers. The sun set on hundreds of windows.

More than twenty years later, his father, remembering that day, said he'd been amazed at how long he was able to carry Jeremiah that way, big as he'd grown. It was like he'd summoned impossible reserves of strength, he said.

Tavern on the Green appeared, its stained-glass windows and big red awning and carriage horses parked out front. They could almost see where the park ended.

"Daddy?"

"Yes, baby?"

"I love you."

His dad was quiet. Then he said, "I thought you wouldn't love me until you were five."

"I couldn't wait."

His father stopped. He let Jeremiah's legs drop, held him under the arms with both hands, and kissed him hard on the head. His father held him tight, tighter than he liked, but Jeremiah loved him.

ACKNOWLEDGMENTS

First I'd like to thank my parents, Jan and Lloyd Constantine, for supporting me while I wrote *Jeremiah's Ghost*. Without them, this book would never have been written, and I'll always be grateful for that, to say the least. I love you both.

Thanks to Michelle Dotter, my editor, for her acuity, the care and respect with which she handled my work, and her faith in this novel, which waited five years for the perfect hands. Briah Skelly, Nick Sinatra, Alison Crellin and Mark Pearce at MP Publishing have all worked hard to make this long and circuitous dream a reality, too, and each deserves credit.

I'm deeply grateful for my dear friend, Stephanie Sesame Campbell, who believed in me and supported me publicly when very few people would. Thanks for your love and compassion.

My warmest and humblest regards to Laura Albert, Jim Shepard and Binnie Kirshenbaum for their generous blurbs. Each was a mentor to me at different stages in my career. It's a wonderful honor to have their support for my debut novel.

I should mention my writing peers and professors at Williams and Columbia who challenged and encouraged my work in the early going. And last, but never least, my friends and readers on Facebook for their attention and time—rare gifts for a writer in this day and age—which I can never return, only hope to reward.

www.ingramcontent.com/pod-product-compliance
Lightning Source LLC
Chambersburg PA
CBHW061448210726

48287CB00007B/2419